For Terry
and Anne,
these looked
interesting.
Enjoy!

And Other Fiction By
Randeane Tetu

Papier-Mache Press Watsonville, California

First Edition
ISBN: 0-918949-13-0 Paperback
ISBN: 0-918949-17-3 Hardcover

Printed in the United States of America

Design by Cynthia Heier
Cover art "Chester Center Spring Morning" © 1991 by Leif Nilsson
Typography by Metro Typography

Thanks and acknowledgement to the following magazines and anthologies for original publication of works included in this collection: *The Calusa Review, The Cutting Edge, Gambit Magazine, Literary Lights, Loonfeather, The Massachusetts Review, Minnesota Review, New England Sampler, Oktoberfest, Oxford Magazine, Z Miscellaneous,* and *The Tie That Binds* (Papier-Mache Press). Special thanks to John R. Jones for reading all my early words and letting me read his.

Library of Congress Cataloging-in-Publication Data

Tetu, Randeane, 1949–
    Merle's & Marilyn's mink ranch and other fiction / by Randeane Tetu.—1st ed.
        p. cm.
    ISBN 0-918949-17-3 (alk. paper) : $14.00 — ISBN 0-918949-13-0 (pbk. : alk. paper) : $9.00
    1. New England—Fiction.   I. Title.   II. Title: Merle's and Marilyn's mink ranch and other fiction.
PS3570.E86M47   1991
813′ .54—dc20   91-33920
                                                              CIP

To John & Emrys
& Katherine the Great

CONTENTS

LET THE OLD CAT DIE DOWN

They will not convince me that the collision with the lion was not deliberate. No one can just drive into a lion without aiming at it. A white lion on a still night when the roads are dry. Louise stabbed her chin down, to punctuate what she had not said out loud, pulling out of Emily's fist the grasp of hair Emily was brushing. *Norman just painted those lions like marble again, and somebody knocked one over last night. A car knocked over one of the lions. Not somebody. A car knocked over one of the two marble lions who watch the road, white with sparkles like maple sugar candy.*

When she had been twenty-four, she had been in Mason's car and seen the lions and had called, "Stop," and Mason had stopped, and she had gone to one lion and patted him and told him, "What a fine lion," before getting into the car with the young man again and not looking at the old age home.

Emily, standing behind her and brushing her hair, said, "The lion's down." *As if I could not see the lion backwards on the ground. As soon as I could see where he wasn't, I could certainly see where he was. Emily only tells me things I already know. My parents did the same thing. That's how they'll get me to let go after a while. Just keep watering it down and after a while I'll forget whether I'm in life or just watching, and when I stop making those distinctions, I'll just slip away.*

Louise remembered suddenly that she knew how to drive a car. "Where's my car?" she asked Emily.

"Your car? Why, I don't know anything about a car, Mrs. Alcott. It certainly isn't here." *They only hired Emily because she said, "I don't know," so I'll have no way of finding out how sharp I still am.* Louise flashed her bright quick fingers into her hair and rewound the bun and pricked the pins into where they would hold something. Then she went for a walk.

The lion on his back had rusty metal bolts sticking straight out under his paws and hindquarters. He was a sitting lion. He looked just pushed over, not damaged.

Louise remembered the fire sirens in the dark of last night.

This morning she walked away from the lions along the wall to the driveway and went down the driveway past the hedge, between the green lawns, to the three-car garage. One door of the garage was missing, and she looked through the doorway at the tangle of brown and aging things. The dump rake in the back with its high wheels, the piled bushel baskets, the rakes and hoes looked familiar, looked as the old carriage shed at home had looked with the hay rake which Grandpa had painted the color of all the leftover farm paints stirred together.

Louise looked in at the doorway. She was a child and ran to her grandfather. He leaned on the vise in the barn where his hands, from touching things, smelled of oil and metal. He smoked cigarettes down to the brown ends and threw the ends into the wheel ruts outside the double barn doors and pushed hard on her swing in the swinging breeze of her until he said, "Let the old cat die down," and wouldn't push her anymore and the swing died down.

Then the other kids were there and they ran across the lawn and back in the magic of the night full of sparklers, writing their names in the sky, in the heavy dark so much deeper than day. They twirled around to make themselves dizzy and lay on the ground to look at the circling sky and see secrets which as a child she'd remembered for a while and then left behind.

At the home, the one car that belonged there was getting old in the garage. Mrs. Georges only sent Norman out to the paint store or the hardware, and when he came back, he backed it into its place.

Cliff Totten, when he'd been caretaker, had always driven the car. But Norman sometimes drove his own truck so Louise couldn't tell by looking for the car if Norman was there or not the way she could have with Cliff. Norman, when he moved into the apartment under the main building next to the kitchen, moved Cliff's stacks of magazines in boxes to the back of his truck and peddled them to Reggie who ran the secondhand furniture store and got a quarter apiece for the old ones. Norman's pickup truck had a camper back. Mrs. Georges didn't like it, but Norman went camping for two days whenever he felt like it.

Louise crossed the lawn behind the home and made a square corner to follow the side stone wall back to the road. Some days she walked away from the home, but today she turned left and followed the wall back to the lions and looked under the fallen one at the bolts, more intriguing and obscene than his lion parts would have been.

When she went onto the porch and looked through the screen door, she heard and saw that the mailman had been and told them about the fire.

She turned and walked back out and passed the lions a third time and turned right toward the center of town. She had heard the sirens. She wouldn't tell them anything either.

People were everywhere on the sidewalks in the center of town, and then she could see the fire trucks, and then she could see the church made of stone, burned and changed with the windows gone and black stains on the stone. She looked at its solid shadow. People moved on the lawn, not hurrying, just looking, and the firemen moved the hoses on the grass.

She stopped walking and stood away from the church lawn thinking how a fire always took away the day and the time. Only later someone would think to say when it happened and that day would be unreal, set apart from real time by the catastrophe and the absence of habit.

She watched the men wind the hoses back onto the truck and the knot of men around the fire marshal break apart. The firemen pulled themselves onto the two trucks which moved slowly away from the front of the building. She saw on the lawn the marks of where they had been the night before.

Across the street from the church was the post office. Louise walked inside to the smell of letters, passion and ink, and the feel of the slick marble that would chill her to touch, and sat on a bench where she could see John Brown lead the slaves to freedom across the upper wall.

In the post office Louise imagined that all the old letters flew from one end of the room to the other, like birds flying down off the telephone wires together and then up and circling back. Watching the letters, she was a small girl who climbed into the haymow at her grandmother's in the rain with the neighbor who lost her bracelet there. She wondered what happened to all the things ever lost in a haymow. The hay dust they stirred into the air made them sneeze and she could not lie still long enough for the tiny crackling straw noises to completely stop around her. Early in the spring she found where the kittens had been in the smooth grey-furred nest, still warm, from which Maida had moved them. She could look down through the back of where the haymow stepped up to the other level to see the stall below with the wheelbarrow and some of the hay that had fallen or been pushed through. From the haymow, she could push her legs through the space and wiggle them in the clear air below while all around would be the dust and the heat stirred up. The neighbor had shot right through there one day, had slid on the slippery hay at the edge to disappear suddenly and without sound in the crackling and breaking of the hay all around, and had had to go out through the barnyard to climb again up the tractor wheel and up the rope from the barn below.

The pictures, sharp in contrast to the later ones of house and family, replaced the grainy images of her middle years with the satisfying clarity of her early ones.

"Hear the fire alarm last night, Mrs. Alcott?" The postmaster, a polite young man whose name she would remember, leaned through the opening above the drawer of stamps, his elbows on the marble.

"Oh, I sleep on the other side from town." *I will not tell them anything.* "What started it going?"

"Hard to say. Hard to say. Fire marshal says could have been anything. Some bad wiring. Some spontaneous combustion."

"Well, it wasn't lightning like took the Millworks because there wasn't any."

"No. Not lightning. Started low down. First floor he thinks."

"Well, you wouldn't think that stone could burn, but look at the doors and all."

"That's the thing. The floor and pews were mostly gone and the heat blew the windows out before anyone even saw it. Lot of destruction. I guess it was Ely called the fire trucks after midnight when his cat had to go out."

"Well, you never think on a day like this there can be destruction. It always surprises you. Has the mailman gone out already with my mail?"

"Yuh. He's gone out with the mail." No one had sent her any mail since she had moved to the home and given up the house where she had lived alone since her husband died.

Louise married her husband because he didn't expect anything out of the ordinary while she worked in the library part-time and filed onto shelves pieces of other people's lives. She had the one son in her promise not to be too much, though he was a surprise to them both.

Her son had his first accident when he tumbled down the stairs at three, though really the first accident had been his conception, and he chose to keep repeating it, the way he first got his parents' attention. It taught him the power of being hurt. He leaned for danger, wanting not only the scare of death, but maybe death itself if he could reach it and it didn't cost too much.

Her husband answered the phone in the night though she was the one who lay awake to listen for it. And in the minutes that she could hear him on the phone as she lay stiff and cold, she prayed, willing to pay anything not to have to bear the worst things she could imagine. She thought about what she might have, what she might give up to save him, but was never able to imagine herself without the things, snatched them back immediately from the touch of her imagination. She would give up the house, the money, the car, until Harry returned from the black other room and said, "I'll go downtown and get him. He's at the station," or "Small cut and a few stitches at the hospital," and she reclaimed the house, the money, the car. She set them in their places so that she had them to give up another night and hoped that he would be careful and not use up all the worry she had. Harry was the one to dress and drive into the night as she lay hard and cold and waited for the car to come home.

So, when she heard of the final accident when he was twenty, alone on a motorcycle in the rain, on a road just starting to slick, she felt some grief and some relief, but she felt also slightly cheated, having saved some worry for the next times which now would not come.

After the crash, now that he was cleanly dead and not battered or broken somewhere, she worried vaguely, using up the love or anger she had been afraid to use when it might have done some good, but which later could do nothing.

Harry would come in with the gunmetal smell of out-doors on him in the fall. After the car rides in the dark were over, he started having the heart trouble which eventually killed him. She could not easily let him go, but imagined sometimes that he was still there, so that when he was not, it was as if he were only staying clear of the back door, not as if he were really gone.

Her husband for forty years, she had wanted to think only of him at his burying, to review like a parade, the moments in their lives that she had noticed for their beauty or their pageantry or their amount of work, but she thought of the preacher who had said words about her son's life and death.

And she could see her son that night on the curve. If the son was too much for Harry, he had never agreed not to be, had never promised anything, had not lived for his father or for her, but had lived always looking for the sweet thrill of the near-death or the death. It didn't matter which.

And then the service finished. "There's a dyin', there's a birth," Harry's sister said to her as they turned and began along the aisle they had come down this far, though as Louise had always heard it, "There's a birth, and there's a dyin'," and they walked from the twilight and the hush.

When she left her husband's house, she gave up easily what had no real attachment and saved some memories between book pages of other lives and let the rest just set-tle behind her. She found some black and white again in the safety of old age at the lion rest home where Mason Dowling had stopped when she was twenty-four to let her pet the lions.

Mason Dowling's hair, full of energy and spark, swept up and back from his face as if sprung there by the sharp drafts of music he flung from a banjo with an Indian painted on it. He looked for old songs at the library where he shifted piles of brown and dusty books from the corners of the upstairs rooms. He kept interested in the soft dusty rearrangement of piles while he courted her. He sang her the song about cats with a lot of meowling.

This home, more like a house than the modern homes where they had everything on soft rubber wheels, had only the five of them, women who could move about on their own and think, though Louise sometimes wondered about Clara. On good days, Clara stitched things together in tiny stitches, but on bad days she tore them out again. Margaret wrote letters and copied them over to mail the next day. Marta and Greta had rooms on the second floor and often went out to see friends whom they talked about at dinner.

After lunch, Louise walked back to the church which looked still and broken in the heat of the sunlight. She sat on the bench in the post office and this time the postmaster said that Mason Dowling's jewelry store had been robbed—the store where Harry had bought their wedding rings and where Mason had fixed links in her bracelets until his wife had left him several years ago and he'd given the store to his son who didn't have the same care for a broken bracelet as his father.

"Yuh. And now they say that fire was set to cause a ruckus so the jewelry store could be robbed," the postmaster told her.

Louise moved to the bench in front of the post office and watched the people come to look at the church.

Mason Dowling turned the corner from the jewelry store and came along the sidewalk. For a moment she thought of the loss of his wife, a younger woman he had married after she had married Harry, gone and left him for a younger man. He must miss the company. He moved more slowly than he had the last time she'd seen him and looked sideways at the church before coming to sit beside her, carefully, as if taking note of how everything went down so he would be able to call it back up when he was ready. "Morning, Louise."

"Morning, Mason. I was sorry to hear about the store."

"Yup. Thank you. I do what I can, but it grieves me."

"Surprised to see you out. I'd heard you weren't feeling well."

"Haven't felt well since Lettie left and that's the truth. But what am I going to do? Store burglarized. I can't keep out of the way. I told Kevin this morning, soon as I heard, that I'd be down to help him. Then I'll go to the police station this evening and go over inventories for Kal."

"Postmaster says the fire was set to draw attention from breaking and entering."

"I suppose he's right. Breaks your heart though to see a beautiful church like that. There's never a reason good enough for that. Nobody noticed the store alarm though."

Across the lawn a group of people gathered to start into the church. "How did they get into the store?" Louise asked him.

"Kal says it was probably one person went in through the back door. Clipped the back corner of the building going out. Kal says everybody knows the store's closed today and nothing was going on at the church after morning service. Kevin found out this morning and called Kal right away.

"Broke in with an ice chopper Kal found leaning up against the back of the store. He figured the car parked between the buildings back from the road. Piece of the back corner was chipped. Looked like black paint. He thinks the alarm went off for a while at least. But somebody cut it off. Anyway, in the noise downtown no one called, or anyway reached Kal until he got back from the fire. And then somebody only said that a car had hit something and kept going. Course the other sirens were going and all."

Breaking and entering, she thought, through the same door her son had broken in to take whatever it was he'd needed, which he didn't find there either to fill the space he'd saved for it, whatever he felt he had coming to him, whether it was the love he missed or the punishment, she couldn't tell.

But by the time Kal had come to the house that time, her son had decided to save what he already had, and denied having been near the jewelry store, though that's when she knew he had. Since the counter had merely been swept clean of displays in a large angry gesture which landed them on the floor and since nothing had been taken, Kal had not come back.

Mason must have known at the time, more than twenty years ago, could even have been thinking of it, when he said, "Hello, Louise," on the bench on this side of their lives.

The night before she had heard voices on the roof. In the dark in the clear moment that she woke knowing that the moment before she had heard what had caused her to wake, she lay flat and unmoving, her eyes wide in the dark, hearing nothing except the infinitesimally small sinking of the home into itself, far from the distinct voices she had just heard.

Now I lay me down to sleep. She saw now the oblong lighter window and curtains and almost the stars, heard the roof but not the voices, and then the fire sirens screamed. The sirens screamed, and she sat up in bed until the noise of her own pounding settled down. *I must stay right here in bed.* And she lay carefully back into the safety of the pillow.

I shouldn't be walking about in the middle of the night. I'm an old lady. She put her raincoat over her night dress and wore her bedroom slippers so she didn't have to put on stockings.

The night was clear except for the noise. Soft petals were blowing from the dogwood trees. Flakes of white floated to the lawn. She stood a long time on the porch but no light came on in the house. She stepped from the porch down the walk to where the lions guarded the entrance.

Along the street she could hear the noise from the center of town. Fire engines beat up Main Street and the sirens dropped to a stop. Lights flew around the darkness. She stopped on the sidewalk to watch people and then she saw the fire burst shooting upward, and with a sigh, people moved back. In the moving and the shouts and what she now saw of the flames from the church, the fire fighters ran out their hoses and the watchers closed in again, and the water hit the roof, and hitting the stone where it did, added loudness to the night. The fire beat a hollow sound, and the water pounded.

Looking up at the night, she saw very real trees above her, very pointed stars. The crowd surged when the flame leaped up and soughed when the water beat it back. The sky circled. Someone was in a tree watching the fire. No one noticed the fourteen-year-old girl she felt she was on the sidewalk in bedroom slippers.

She went back up the street and waited a long time on the porch to see if the lights would go on.

Up from town a car came quickly past, spraying car noise onto the porch. She saw the taillights redden as the car stopped. In a moment, the white back-up light came on, and the car backed around, and swung the headlights across the dogwood tree as it faced town and came back slowly. The car lurched to hit the first lion, and Louise jumped up, and the car backed off and turned around again and sped away from town.

Louise got up from the bench and said good-bye to Mason. Walking back from town, she looked in treetops, looking to find herself, she thought, in a picture she had thought to keep and lost before she knew it, and looked for again all her life.

Norman was just heaving a rolled sleeping bag through the driver's side window of his truck, and suddenly she saw that he was leaving, that he had taken the car from the garage and knocked the corner of the jewelry store and bumped into the lion to cover the dent. The idea quickened through her. Norman went back into the building below her. She had to pass the truck on her way to the garage.

She fit in between where the lawn mower was parked and the edge of the door jamb where the door was missing, and got into the second bay where an old refrigerator stood with hay bales around it. Bales had been left clear of the door to fit a dining room table, and she crawled over the top of it on her knees to reach the third bay where the car had been driven in. She went around the paint cans and opened the driver's side door. The courtesy light came on and she found the key in the ashtray where she had expected to find it, where Mrs. Georges insisted that Norman leave it after it had been misplaced so many times.

She had thought it would be backed in, but then she thought it made sense that it wasn't since Norman would not have wanted to leave that dented front facing out, and now she would have to back it up. The shift was on the wheel and she would only need reverse and low to get it out and up the driveway. She could see well enough in the dusk of the garage to leave off the lights. The car started easily though she had never driven this car before. She left it in neutral to open the garage door, and then she backed into the shade in the turnaround.

The driveway climbed to the road with the lawns higher on each side up to the low stone wall and a hedge. Only the driveway left space to the road.

Louise shifted into low and aimed between the hedge and the wall. Her head pounded with sound. She gave the car too much gas and it took forever to let out the clutch. The car moved up the driveway, past Norman's truck which headed downhill. Norman was still inside. Just after the hedge, Louise turned right past the stone wall and stopped. She put in the clutch and rolled back to the hedge and stopped the car almost completely across the driveway.

She turned off the ignition, let out the clutch, and put the key into her shoe. She saw Norman get into his truck. He hadn't looked at her, and she left the car and went between the lions and climbed the porch and went inside to call Kal.

Norman pulled down in front of the garage to back around. He stopped the truck when he saw where the car was, hauled on the emergency brake, and climbed out. He walked to the car, climbed into the driver's seat, and, after a minute, not finding the key, jumped out quickly, and though she could not see him do this, she knew he would run around the front of the car, around the dented fender that she hadn't thought to look for she was so sure that it was the same car she had watched the night before run into one of the lions.

She said into the phone, "I knew it was my son, but now it's Norman. It isn't my son anymore," and thought now Mason could hold her as if she were young, now that she had told him.

Because she held the phone, she couldn't watch while Norman jumped into the truck again and pulled the door, and slammed into reverse, and backed again, and slammed into first, and jumped the truck up the lawn right onto the walk, and aimed between the lions where the first one was down. She could tell by the noise, though on the other end of the line Kal just said, "Okay, Mrs. Alcott."

Louise saw from the phone, as Norman must see from the truck, that the space between the lions wasn't wide enough. But he ran the left front tire up the fallen lion and onto the stone plinth. The back tire missed the lion as a ramp and the front tire went off the plinth and the body of the truck came down hard and jarring on the stone with the front wheel above the ground and the back wheel against the stone.

Seeing it against the blank wall of her mind and thinking it made up for the compromises she had made coming

13

through life, Louise waited a moment without hanging up the phone receiver, holding it in her thumb and fingers just above the cradle where she couldn't hear the dial tone. She waited, watched the police car come slowly out from town and stop and Mason get out the other side and come across the street and up the porch to her while her heart pounded a way she didn't think it could.

She put the receiver down and went out onto the porch. She remembered that Norman was going camping and then saw that the car had no dents and that Norman's truck hadn't moved. Kal's car came up the street and he stopped it slowly.

It could have been Norman. She had moved the car as if it had been Norman. Now she lay in the dark after the sparklers, starting off into sleep twirling to the right.

The shooting rocket sparks echoed in her vision. Under the stars on a side lawn she slid off on the start of a spin, *Let the old cat die down, now I lay me down to sleep*, and pictured Mason coming around the car and up to her on the porch.

THE CONVOY

T he generator that powered the sign for the bridge rattled and barked through the day and kept Marjorie awake at night. The highway department sign had a light behind the white glass and black letters that marked out—Road Narrows. The sign was directly in front of her rose bushes. The noise made her feel hearing impaired, and she felt a thunderstorm coming down the river. The air had weight to it.

Inside the house, the sound of the idling engine made her feel that a convoy truck was waiting out in front. Waiting to let all the men out onto her lawn or waiting to pick her up, she couldn't tell. She had seen a convoy truck like it one summer of her life. The back was covered with tarp, and she couldn't see, but she thought the men were inside, sitting on benches down both sides of the back of the truck. The truck stayed parked in front of her rose bushes.

She took the clippers and went out to cut roses for the table. The orange struts held the sign, harsh and straight, to the generator which weighted the sign to the lawn. It looked like government property. It was all out of proportion, she thought, to the bridge they were repairing. Traffic could pass in both directions even though the lane where the men were working was closed. Down the road almost a mile, the crew working on the bridge would be talking, moving shovels toward their trucks, wrapping their shirts around their necks to leave for the day.

No cars went past while she was cutting the pink-petaled roses. She broke off the thorns on the stems she'd cut so they didn't press into her hand. When Harry came they didn't have supper on the porch because of the noise.

"Everyone gone home from the bridge?" Marjorie said.

"Gone home. Can't see any difference from last week. When did they bring your sign?"

"Yesterday," she said. "Brought it and swung it out of the truck on a chain hitched to the plow of one of their bulldozers."

"Keep you awake?"

"Yes, it does."

"Welcome to come to my place."

Marjorie looked straight at him after he said that. Harry reminded her of her first husband who had died in the war. Roy had left and died early. Harry looked nothing like him, but Marjorie thought that if Roy had lived this long he might be much like Harry.

It suddenly seemed more true to her that had Roy lived he would not have attained the sense of confidence and quiet energy that Harry had developed. Harry had brought up his family and lost his wife. In the last two years he had come once a week for supper with her. He brought chocolates or wine, and in the winter, flowers.

The storm was rolling closer and the air pressed in around them, making her feel that she and Harry were cut out of the air and sitting how they must sit. Then she moved, stood to go for the coffee.

"Thank you," she said. "But I keep feeling I'm still married." She could hear Roy's convoy truck out past the rose bushes, waiting. She smiled, admitting to herself and to Harry that it was a silly way to feel. Harry smiled, and, watching him slope back into the air that pressed around them, she saw that he had meant it, had wanted her to say yes.

The man she felt married to was very young and Harry was her own age. She brought the coffee and filled their cups.

Harry let the weight of the air sit on the table between them and she watched him, quietly, through it. At nine she walked him to the door and he kissed her good-night.

Rain was close down on the river. She watched his truck leave, the taillights fuzzy in the thickened air. Then she shut off the house lights and got into bed.

A convoy truck was stopped in front of her house. Her husband was in the truck but they wouldn't let her see him. She couldn't get up onto the truck through the canvas flaps at the back, and he couldn't climb down to her on the ground. She hid in the rose bushes and the thorns grasped her arms. Roy was young, peeking, with the others, out the back flaps where they wouldn't let him get down, and they wouldn't let her climb up.

He was young, the way he'd been young the last time she'd seen him. She was afraid she looked very ugly to him now that she was fifty-eight. She must look older than his mother the last time he'd seen his mother. Marjorie reached the roses up to him, and he passed down a coin from his pocket. She saw he didn't know her. He thought she was an old woman cutting roses. He hadn't seen she was still young and waiting for him.

The sign banged in the night. Marjorie lay flat and cold in her bed. The rainstorm came. Lightning flashed in all the windows, and thunder rolled over the noise of the sign. Rain came in the east window and she lay in bed.

She waited for the storm to pass. It was over before one o'clock and she called Harry on the phone.

When he came, they took the stone boat from the back of his truck and, with the chain hitched to the truck, pulled the sign and generator onto it. The ground was not too soft from the rain, but the grass was slippery.

They worked in the light that the generator made, throwing power through the bulbs behind the white glass. Then Marjorie sat in the cab with him, and Harry pulled the stone boat along the road for half a mile. He unhitched the chain from the stone boat and hitched it to the sign and, with the truck, dragged it onto the grass. There was no house. It was a quarter mile to the bridge. No cars passed them.

The generator threw white light through the glass, out-lining the loud black letters. Harry hitched the chain to the stone boat again and pulled it back to Marjorie's drive-way, and left the truck to take Marjorie inside. He stayed. In bed Marjorie lay awake for a while and heard the sound of the convoy truck far away, leaving, leaving.

THE BLIND SIDE

Harvey walked everywhere, and where he didn't walk he drove. He drove a pale blue Pinto with one door. The door on the driver's side was missing, so when he drove, he drove what looked like a cutaway car rigged to demonstrate highway safety. He had a tendency to look out the open door instead of through the windshield when he drove—it was so much more open, so much bigger. And he had a tendency to steer to the left. Anyone watching would see the seat depressed on its springs, his legs reaching down to the pedals, and the way he tended to look out the door at the world that pressed in on the left.

He was only in the car when he wasn't walking, and there wasn't much he couldn't walk to. He walked to the post office to get his mail. He walked to the library, grocery store, barber shop.

When he drove, he drove across the fields after they'd been mown, or he drove to the lake at the state park and parked the car and walked around in the woods.

At Harvey's house, Stipples had put building paper over half of the windows. Harvey had all the lights on and it seemed just like night, wrapped in. At night, when he was in the side of the house that still had its windows, he felt even those windows had building paper, and he wouldn't look at them.

He was trying to think of a place to walk, but he wouldn't walk to Seven Maples because last night Hobie Alston had told him, "You look like you've lost weight. You feel all right?"

"Man my age shouldn't be carrying the weight of a man yours," he told him, but Hobie had had a few beers and kept looking over as if seeing him for the first time and saying, "Gee, you look so pale, you lost weight. You feel all right?" Harvey didn't figure Hobie should be saying anything to him until he paid for the car door. Harvey figured he was too old to deck him, though. Probably twice as old as Hobie who was in his thirties.

Made him feel sort of puny. He'd wait until Monday now. Go back to the Maples and, when he walked in, Muzzy'd tell him, "Hey, where you been keeping yourself? Looking pretty good for an old man." He'd wait over the weekend, let some of Hobie wear off so it'd take when Muzzy said that.

He had to go somewhere tonight though. When he was in one side of the house, it bothered him to get going someplace because it felt as if it was already night. Then when he went to the other side, he was disoriented because it was light so he didn't have to leave yet.

Stipples had been painting the windows right in the house, but when the Almanac said rain, he'd taken them all out of the side he hadn't done and put them into his truck and driven off with them. Harvey'd had to ask Greta at the hardware store to call Stipples and say, "What about the open windows if it's going to rain?"

Greta looked so pretty talking into the phone, looking down at the desk and then flashing her eyes up at him when Stipples said something on the other end. Harvey thought she must have changed her weight or done her hair or something because he had seen her before and she hadn't looked like this. Or he thought maybe having half the windows out of the house might have changed his way of looking at things.

Then Stipples had come back with the windows still in the truck, and cut and tacked up the building paper. From the road the windows were the color of old red rubber erasers and dull. The rain on the building paper sounded soft. When the rain hit the building paper, it made a soft fuzzy noise.

It made Harvey feel that he had a dark side. Stipples had taken the windows away a week ago Thursday.

Harvey walked through the front hall from one side of the house to the other, fuming that he'd promised himself not to go to Seven Maples, and finally went out the front door to the hardware store. It was still afternoon.

"My house is building papered in," he said to Greta. "Maybe you'd like to go for a drive tonight?"

"Excuse me?" she said.

"I said my house is still papered in. Would you like to call Stipples for me?"

"Oh, of course," she said. He thought she looked disappointed. The crease between her eyebrows that she'd had when she was trying to listen smoothed out.

She found Stipples' number and dialed. She looked lovely on the telephone, Harvey thought. Maybe it was that he'd never seen her on the telephone before.

All the time he'd lived in his house, he'd never had a phone put in. "Right in town what do I need one for?" he asked Muzzy. "I need to make a call, I can walk down to the gas station, spend a dime. I don't need to pay by the month."

Greta hung up the phone. "Sorry," she said. "No answer." She looked at the desk.

"Oh, well, how about that drive tonight?" She looked up at him the way she had looked a week ago when Stipples had said something she had to tell him.

"What time?"

"Oh, about eight?" Some people, he thought, look just great on the phone.

She nodded, smiled. "'D be nice," she said. "Where?"

"Oh, just thought we'd drive around."

"No, I mean where should I meet you?"

"Oh, where do you live? I'll pick you up."

"Over the feed and grain," she said, "but I'll meet you in front."

"Sure." He pushed off the counter and walked out and down the street, and when he came in through the front door, he turned and stayed in the open side of the house until he had to go to the kitchen to make supper.

The building paper, when the lights were off, had little stars like the shade in his bedroom had had when he was a little boy taking naps.

It wasn't raining. Harvey didn't take the car out of the garage if it was raining. When he backed it out, the evening had gotten to the point where when he let off the hand brake, he noticed how white his socks were.

Harvey drove to the feed and grain and noticed how white Greta's gloves were. He stopped at the curb and ran around to open the passenger's door for her. He had the car lights on, but when he opened the door, the courtesy light didn't go on. He'd had it disconnected when he'd had the door removed after Hobie backed into it leaving Seven Maples.

The replacement door was at the gas station in a crate, but Harvey wouldn't accept it or pay shipping charges until he and Hobie worked out who was paying for it. So far it wasn't Hobie, so Harvey wouldn't touch the door.

Greta stepped in and Harvey closed her door, went around and got down into his own seat behind the wheel. Greta didn't look at him yet so he drove down the main street, turned off into Hobie's field onto the track the hay truck used going out to the back fields. His headlights hit across the hay stubble and the white moths came up in the headlights.

A moon was starting to go up over the edge of trees on the stone wall. Harvey drove slowly and, when he came to the blueberry bushes, circled the field and started back. He didn't say anything and Greta didn't say anything. He could see the moon out his open doorway.

When he'd first driven the car without the door, after the twin at the garage had taken off the door and disconnected the courtesy light, Harvey'd thought he was apt to fall out. Thought he leaned in that direction much more than he had when the door was on.

He liked to drive out over the fields because they seemed like a soft place to land. He could watch the streaks of motion the grass stubble became moving past his feet and think they looked light enough to hold him up.

Harvey came back toward the road. The two tracks of the hay truck looked lighter than the rest of the field. He came down past Hobie's barn and out onto the road.

"That was nice," Greta said, and he remembered she was there. His body shielded her from the open door. The light-colored sand on the edge of the road skimmed past and the lines in the road that the pebbles made in the motion of the car skimmed past the open door.

Harvey drove out toward the lake in the State Park.

"Moon'll be up on the water," he said and pulled off the road into one of the turnarounds. He stopped the car and turned off the headlights. The night seemed quiet around them, the way a night seems quiet by the water. Harvey slid off the seat and went around to open Greta's door. He took her gloved hand and led the way down toward the lake. There was a beach and there were two benches and a trash can. They sat on the bench nearer the lake and the moon was just over the trees and shining up from the water.

They sat on the bench and Harvey held her gloved hand and the moon was over the trees and down in the water.

Harvey was thinking how closed in he felt in the half of his house with building paper, how it made him want to look out and see what he might be missing and how when he'd looked out he'd seen Greta, and how when there was no door on the driver's side of the car, the world went past so close.

They heard another car pull off the road. They heard some kids talking and going down a path toward the rocks on their left. After a while another car came, and the kids came down onto the beach, saw them and veered around toward the rocks.

"You look so nice on the phone," Harvey said. The lake stretched out in front of them. "How would it be if I got a phone? Call you up and talk sometime?"

"Oh, that'd be nice, I think." He held her gloved hand. They could hear the kids down on the rocks, and then they could see them, jumping out into the water, swimming, and they could hear them calling, the way sound carries at night over water.

"Maybe I should drive you home now," Harvey said.

"Maybe."

He stood up and she stood up with him, looked at the moon and at where the kids were spreading the moon around in the water and walked back to the car.

The next day was Saturday, and while Harvey was at the hardware store, Stipples came with the painted windows and took down the building paper.

THE TROUBLE I'VE SEEN

Nobody knows the trouble I've seen.
Nobody knows but Jesus.

When she was the only passenger on the bus, as she was today, Melanie sat directly behind the bus driver and sang softly for him as if she were singing to herself, at home alone, but so he could hear.

Melanie had her hair set in loops with bobby pins all over her head. It made her forehead look particularly bare and wrinkled and her eyebrows, which were grey rather than brown like the hair in loops, look glued on in the wrong directions.

She had her sweater over her shoulders because the bus was air-conditioned. On the street downtown she would fold it through the handle across her purse and in the stores she would wear it again if she needed it.

She needed hair setting lotion and talcum powder and, if it wasn't too expensive, she'd buy a five-dollar basket. Last week when she had held the basket in her hands it had seemed too much. But today it might not.

"When we had popcorn," she told the bus driver, "I used to bite off all the kernels first and have a handful of just the white fluffy parts. Then I ate those."

"Um-hum." The driver downshifted into the college parking lot and Melanie could see that the young men from Saudi Arabia were at the bus stop shelter. The bus swung and stopped and the doors flapped open. Melanie sat with her hand on the metal bar behind the driver and counted them up the steps. Twenty-two she counted and watched to see if the last one would duck out of the building to come running across the parking lot.

Heat rose in ripples above the parked cars and made

Melanie think of mirages in the desert, of oases and camels. The doors flapped shut. Twenty-two. The other one must be home sick. The Saudis went together everywhere. It was a pact, she thought, a religious pact to keep them safe in this foreign country.

"I swing by, sometimes," the driver had told her. "I see them praying. Right there on the lawn, facing East. Certain times of the day." Melanie hadn't seen them praying. She couldn't tell who was missing. Some of them were tall and some were short. Some had beards. They spoke in gearshift sounds to each other behind her.

"Women in their country, you know, still cover their faces," the driver said to her into the mirror. He pulled the bus onto the road.

French in a soft voice made Melanie think of being loved. The un-English sounds of these young men, though, made her think of fierce and raw destruction, machines and men in fast motion.

Through the tinted glass window Melanie thought of Richard at college before he went back to France. Before he had gone back, Richard had locked them into his car and made love to her behind the brick administration building where the iron fire escape came down to the grass where he parked. In summer the syringa blossoms blew off bushes and through the open car windows and past the night haze in the street light at the corner.

Richard held her across the car seat. She turned her head and felt the words like kisses.

"You don't mind that I make love to you in French," Richard said, every time. The words were his voice telling her things beautiful beyond imagination, too extraordinary for English, and the words moved his hands down her blouse, and the words slid over her skin with his hands. Melanie leaned her breasts forward and turned her head, and the syringa was gone and the window was closed green glass.

The driver said, "What do you want?" and she looked in the mirror at the driver looking past her, and then she turned and saw one of the Saudis standing in the aisle.

The brakes of the bus squeaked and the driver pulled to the side of the road in the heat that fell against the tar.

"Do you want to stop? Get off?"

The Saudi said something to his friends in their language and they laughed and the man said, "It is too cold. We want you please to stop the air condition."

Melanie looked back at the mirror at the driver and he put the bus into gear. He looked down from the overhead mirror to the side view mirrors and pulled the bus onto the road. Melanie watched his head and forehead in the mirror to see when he would change the air conditioner.

Sidewalks hadn't started yet and the bus rolled past empty houses with the grown people off to work and the children off to school. A dog was tied in this heat to the handle of a garage door.

Someone called from the back and Melanie turned. The man was standing. She didn't know whether he had sat down in between.

"Stop," he called. "Yes. We want to stop," and the other men stood up from the seats, but they didn't move into the aisle. The bus slowed, and the men moved behind the first one. The bus stopped, and the doors flapped open.

Melanie turned and looked front. She could see the heat at the open doors but she couldn't feel it yet. She heard the men in the aisle behind her and the bus rocked. They spoke in sharp language.

She felt a breeze of heat and they darkened the bus and went past her and down the steps. Their dark hands held the metal pole and they swung themselves down to the street. The bus driver leaned on his elbow on the steering wheel and watched them go.

Melanie saw their backs and the backs of their heads and when the last one dipped off the step into sunshine, she saw them all again facing the bus, clustered past the door.

The bus driver pulled the lever and the doors flapped together and he checked his side view mirrors.

"Wait," Melanie said. One of the men had stepped in front of the bus and was looking up through the windshield. He waved his arm.

"What?" The driver took his foot off the gas and pulled the gearshift into neutral. "What now?"

Others moved in front of the bus. Lawrence of Arabia, Melanie thought, and suddenly through the window saw the bloodthirsty desert tribes, a train wreck, the bus on its side with arms, legs, torn clothes, and blood out the windows. "Oh," she said and clutched the metal bar behind the driver.

"What do they want?" he said.

"Hostages," she shouted silently at the driver. "Hostages of course. And when they have them . . ."

A tall man rapped his knuckles against the glass and signaled toward the door.

"Don't open," Melanie shouted silently. In the mirror she could see his head and forehead and the driver reached and opened the doors. A man on the ground said, "Come out now. We invite you. Come out."

The driver stayed firm in the seat with his hand on the door lever and then his chest went past the mirror and his shape cut off the outside heat and light and she saw his back in sunshine.

"Yes, you too," the man said to her and, not knowing she had moved, Melanie discovered herself next to the driver in the heat.

"Sometimes," the driver said to her, "through the window, I see them talk and laugh a lot. And sometimes they are quiet."

She kept her eyes focused on the doorway, on the steps past where the doors folded back. She kept from looking at the men. She didn't look at the driver, as if any motion might trigger action.

The men walked around each other, spoke to each other, and someone sang in their language, a keen sound. Heat stripped the layer of cool from her skin and pressed itself against her. She wanted to move her arms to slip the sweater down and fold it over her purse, but she didn't move.

They would next turn the bus on its side, rock it, and with harsh cries tip it over and spill arms and legs out of the windows. She looked at the steps and the dim interior of the bus.

The men moved around each other in their own language and then there was fast motion and Melanie jumped and someone leaped up the bus steps. It was the man who had called the bus to stop. He leaped up the steps of the bus into her vision and swung into the driver's seat. He pulled his eyebrows down over his eyes and scowled at the side view mirrors. He put the bus in gear and turned the wheel. The men around her made harsh calls and someone broke away and climbed through the door and pulled at the man in the seat. The doors banged closed and open and closed. The men called and waved their arms and pushed close to the bus. They called against the closed doors and knocked on the windshield, and then they were laughing and the doors banged open and both men came down into sunlight and the men moved around each other and quickly then, Melanie thought, it happened that they moved away from the doorway and were still.

"We have adjusted for you the temperature," the first man said to the driver. "You may take us please to downtown."

The driver did not look at the men. He looked ahead of him to right and left and Melanie thought he was checking the side mirrors. Then he stepped up to the steps and Melanie began to follow.

The Saudi stepped forward to her. "Give me your hand, beautiful lady," and smiled to her and helped her up the step.

The Saudis crowded at the door and rocked the bus moving down the aisle. Then they were seated and called to each other. The driver closed the doors and pulled the bus onto the road.

In the dimness that was cooler than outside, Melanie tipped her head forward and, self-consciously, pulled the bobby pins out of the front loops and with her fingers combed the hair down to cover her forehead.

I t had rained all night and was raining in the morning. Granite ducked out the house door, opened the car door, stepped into the retired police car, and sank it down onto the grass between the ruts that made the driveway.

The car smelled of carbon paper. Everything Granite wrote he wrote in duplicate, and the type of carbon paper he bought smelled strongly of carbon and green backing. He filed the duplicates into one of the two file cabinet drawers on the back seat. From the front seat he could reach the drawers, but he couldn't look for anything. If he wanted to look for anything, he opened one of the back doors and searched. The A-Z file folders were pushed to the backs of the drawers and in chronological order from back to front were stuffed reports, incoming mail, his tax bills, and letters from his niece. His niece wrote him letters based on the 1962 photo he had sent her of himself in uniform. He answered that, of course, the life he led was dangerous, and sent her examples of the dangers. He kept the duplicates.

Granite started the car and cleared the windshield with the wipers. A trickle ran down the inside of the windshield behind the mirror and lost itself in the dash. He drove down the driveway. The papers on the seat and the box of ink pads and rubber stamps slid forward, and he caught them back. The car scraped over the ridge on the center of the driveway where it came to the road and Granite thought, "Yep, gonna have to smooth that down."

The road was good solid wet and the rain was good steady rain. He drove to Benny's.

"Letter from my niece," he told Louie. "Wants to know why there's only one restaurant in my town."

"Well," Louie said, "I forgot my key this morning and had to pick the back door lock. I thought you'd want to know. What are you going to tell her about the one restaurant?"

"Going to say because you're cooking, Louie. Then I'll describe what you serve. I was going to say, you have a menu I can send along? She gets a kick out of stuff like that."

"How old's this kid now?"

"Oh, I don't know. I was twenty-four when she was born so that would make her, let's see. I was born . . . so . . . she's twenty-three. No, she can't be. She'd be grown up. I was born . . . My sister was . . ."

Louie sipped his coffee. "What you're saying, you been writing to her long enough now you're writing to a grown woman. Don't be surprised when you get an invitation to her wedding."

"But I got a picture here." Granite took his wallet from his breast pocket. "She's just the cutest . . ." He dug a picture from the brittle plastic.

"When was that taken though?"

"Why . . . just a couple years ago."

Louie took the picture. "Well, it's a cinch she doesn't look like that now."

Granite stepped under the rain from the roof into the rain slapping the car and ducked inside. The car settled on its tires, and he closed the door. He turned the ignition. What, he was thinking, can I write to this woman? I never was good at writing letters. I never know what to say. I never know what they're interested in. What they want to hear. Maybe I should write just one last letter. He turned off the main road, drove out Four Mile Sister, looked along at the fields, wet in the rain, the stone walls. Say I've just discovered, I have just made the alarming discovery, that you are, must be a . . . grownup. Hm. Discovered. Child Bride Sends Wedding Invitations.

Four Mile Sister stopped, and he turned onto Hog's Hill. It was a steady rain that bent down the weeds and brush and darkened the spaces between trees. She probably wants to know the best apples for apple pies and the secrets to a man's heart. She probably shows my letters to her friends and they laugh. She is grown up. They think I'm ridiculous.

Granite kept driving. He turned automatically at the end of Hog's Hill. The windshield wipers slapped rain off the windshield. The car smelled of carbon paper.

She only writes me letters to goad me on. She thinks I'm funny. Rain entered the car and settled in his chest, made him breathe four tough sobs. I'm not very brave, he thought. I am quite ridiculous. I can't write her any more. I can't write her knowing what she thinks of me. He stuck his chin out at the window. Expose myself to mockery. Just to amuse her friends.

No. Not even one last letter, he thought. That would be too much. She will write maybe once or twice and then figure I have died in the call of duty, slain by an assassin's bullet, overcome by a gang of criminals I sent up. And the letters will stop coming, and she can make apple pies and forget me.

He hit his fist against the steering wheel and frowned through the windshield. He lifted the weight out of his pocket and stopped the car in the road. Granite took the picture from the wallet and looked at it. The girl had blonde hair in two ponytails on the sides of her head. Well, he said, aren't you the cutest . . . His mouth began to smile. Well, it was a few years ago, he decided. Her hair might be a little longer. He put the picture on the steering wheel, held it with his thumb. He drove the car through Widow-maker Curve.

Louie forgot his key, Granite said to himself, and he had to let himself in the back door. He was leaned over in the rain wearing, already, the white apron wrapped around

him and leaning over, he started reeling off the movie picture, and describing it in words.

He pulled the car to the side of the road. He dug lined
paper and a carbon from the box and pile on the seat and
started, Dear Ellen. Rain dripped from the trees, thunked
onto the hood and roof of the car.

Granite wrote the headline:

MAN APPREHENDED BREAKING INTO RESTAURANT

He described the morning. 7:20. I had just come onto
the main road—I have to fix the hump in the driveway,
Granite thought—when some sixth sense told me to turn
toward Benny's. He described Louie and how he reacted to
the weight of the hand of the law on his shoulder. "A
harmless local seeking shelter from the rain," he ended.

Granite filed the duplicate and folded the original into
an envelope. Maybe I shouldn't stamp the koala bears, he
thought. Hell, she gets a kick out of that. He pressed the
koala bears onto the ink pad and stamped them onto the
corner of the envelope.

An Afterimage of Stars

Alexis had the chain saw and the axe on the trailer with the firewood she was bringing in. She drove the tractor along the ruts and looked to each side of the trail. Off the trail were open spaces. Sunlight struck through the tall trees onto the smaller trees and made the tops of them bright. In an open space, sunlight struck onto a shillelagh. Alexis stopped the tractor and set the brake.

Whatever vine had grown around the young tree and twisted it had died and dropped off and left the tree in its twisted shape as if a snake were coiled around it.

Alexis took the chain saw and went through the brush at the trail edge. The shillelagh was a young tree. She cut it down and cut off the branches to make a staff eight feet long. She put the shillelagh and the chain saw onto the wood on the trailer.

The tractor was idling, and Alexis climbed up, let off the brake, and pushed the gas forward. Coming in from the woods she wasn't thinking anything in particular. She jogged on the tractor seat as the tractor pulled over the ruts and the trailer followed.

"There's magic in a shillelagh," her grandfather had told her when she was a little girl and he'd brought her a tiny shillelagh and a lady's slipper from the woods. There's magic in a shillelagh, Alexis was thinking as she came in. She was thinking, too, of how the Masonic Lodge had a vaulted ceiling papered over with blue paper and silver stars. When her grandfather used to go in to clean there, taking his brown Stanley vacuum from home, he had taken her with him. "These are special ceremonies go on here," he'd said. "And you must respect that." The stars climbed the vaulted blue ceiling. She knew he meant it was magic, like the shillelagh.

After her grandfather died, Alexis took his brown Stanley vacuum and cleaned the lodge. She could feel the power of the ceremonies held in the air by the walls and ceiling. The stars pressed down. When she had dust-mopped the walls, dusted the window sills, and vacuumed the floor, Alexis sat on the floor and watched the ceiling. Between her and the stars she tried to see the magic and the power that was there. She sometimes fell asleep, curled on the floor, and she sometimes danced to music she heard from the ceiling. Then she took the vacuum and locked the door and went home.

Alexis brought the load of firewood in behind the barn. Now that she was sixteen, she sometimes stayed the night at her grandfather's house. She missed what he had shown her, what he had said. Her father was in a daze all the time as if he had his mind on something far away. He'd been this way as long as she could remember, and Alexis had always had the feeling that it was something left from his days in the service. "How does he work?" she had asked her mother. "He's employed to think," she had said. "And he does it very well." Her mother got him into the car in the morning, and out of habit, he arrived at work on time.

Without her grandfather, Alexis felt adrift. It was a good time to stay at his house. Her mother kept running out to Aunt Jo's. Aunt Jo had had a hard time delivering her baby. "They've got to name her soon," her mother said, "or she'll get some name like Pumpkin or Honey.

"Your father had you named before you were born," she said. "Alexis for some old flame, I think, and Alexandra after me."

"You go ahead to Aunt Jo's," Alexis had said. "I'll stay a couple of nights at Grandpa's."

"You stay there if you want, but there's that picnic at the Stevens' house. You plan to go, Alexis. Your dad will be there and I'm sending baked beans. Stevens is going to unveil that wooden Indian he carved from the pine Grandpa gave him. You go."

Alexis put the chain saw and the axe into the woodshed and the shillelagh inside the door to the house. Then she unloaded the firewood she'd cut.

She washed up in Grandpa's old tub and put on the clothes she'd brought and walked over to Stevens'.

Her father was already there. She saw him as she came around the lilac bushes onto the stones, but he didn't see her. Stevens came up right away as if he'd been watching for her.

"Oh, how tall are you?" he said. "You have the right-sized face."

"For what?" she said.

"For the next Indian. I'm working on that other piece of pine your granddad gave me. Thought it was free of knots when I started, but then, see, I found a knot in her fore-head. Right there in the middle. Nothing to do about it, see, except take it off. Took off the whole face. So now I can carve one, glue it on."

"What about checks?" she said. "Don't you have to dry it pretty carefully?"

"Oh, checks. It checks. Lets you know it isn't plastic. Right-sized face you have, though, deep-set eyes. Thing is you do it straight, too straight, right on the line, ends up looking Egyptian. Have to be careful or the Indian looks Egyptian. What can I get you?" He took her over to the table where he had soda and liquor and ice. "There it is," he said and pointed to something standing wrapped in a bed sheet and tied with cord.

"Took my wife's measurements exactly, raised the bust, smoothed out the hips. Hey, I figure, I'm doing the carv-ing, carve it the way I like it." He fixed her a soda on ice, fixed a drink for his wife and went to find her.

The other Indian, standing, had a counterpane draped

over it for the unveiling. Alexis moved to stand in front of it and tried to picture what the pine log Grandpa had given him would look like as an Indian. But she could only picture an Egyptian.

Behind her she heard her father's voice and looked around to see the back of his head, the drink in his hand. He was talking to Angie Tobin and saying, "Lovely people." She could see he was looking past the woman's head. "You're right," he said. "They're the loveliest people. I must tell you. When I went into the service I thought they must ship me to Japan. But Japan was almost over, you know, and they sent me to the Appalachians. Met my first wife lost in the hills with an Army jeep. Get over one of those bridges and you can't tell one road from another, or find the bridge you came over on to get back. I was lost, not she. Stayed there five years. One of the finest persons I've ever met. My first wife, Alexis. It took me five years to leave, but I left finally. You see, we didn't have children and I wanted a girl. When we got married Alexandra said, "Okay, we'll keep trying until we get your girl. Got her first try though. Most men want boys, I think."

Alexis stood in front of the wooden Indian waiting to be unveiled. I'm sixteen, she was thinking, and he never said he had a wife. If there's a knot in her forehead, nothing to do but take off the face.

She didn't stay. She walked home to Grandpa's and got out the shillelagh she'd cut and carried it like a staff to the Masonic Lodge and unlocked the door with the key from the window ledge. Inside it was not quite dark and light reflected up from the ground in through the windows. The air was thick with power. Alexis thought about her first mother Alexis and her second mother Alexandra and it seemed to her it had taken the two of them to make her. Her father was lost over a bridge that he couldn't cross back.

She sat on the floor and held the shillelagh across her lap. She tipped her head up to the vaulted ceiling covered with stars on blue paper. After she looked at them long enough there was a background of shadow stars, bluer than the blue of the ceiling and shifting silently behind the silver ones.

I should know better than to stand on the wood like that. It'll roll on you. But there's a fool at any age, even eighty-six. Now I should know enough to close the draft to come out here. Did I? I didn't? No, I checked the fire and saw the kindling had caught up and I needed this round wood, and shut the door, did I leave it open a crack? No, I don't think so, I left the front open, though, so if it gets sparking, it'll set the rug on fire. It won't get sparking, though. It's going hot and right up the pipe. Well, the pipe could catch then or the chimney. Well, it could, but it never has before and that's good dry wood all year. The lath then.

Dickerson had a fire where the kindling got going so hot with the draft and the damper open that the lath around the pipe under the plaster caught. Yes, but they didn't have a thimble into the chimney. Someone'd just stuck the stove pipe through to the chimney.

Oh, that's right. Well, if it doesn't burn down with me out here, Emmet can get me off from here when he comes. Course the house'll be cold if it doesn't burn.

Eva lay across the wood pile where the round wood had rolled from under her feet.

Don't think I'm hurt. Just awkward getting up is all. Sore in the side here where the wood's poking. Well, Emmet'll be coming. Not too long. Let me see if I can count up the great-grandchildren. She picked out the chopping block and talked to it. Well, there's nineteen with the little one born this week. Someone dies, someone's born, they say. I ain't heard who's died.

She thought for a minute. And it won't be me. I just got a few minutes to hold onto myself here and Emmet'll come haul me off the pile. The possum'll come first. Unless

Emmet's stuck in the mud where the brook runs down at the corner. He could be stuck.'

Then he'll either walk home or he'll get Ralph to hitch him up to the tractor and pull him out. He'll get Ralph to pull him out either way. Then he'll either walk or he'll try again getting through with the car.

Well, it's not awful cold. Warm wind last week to make the mud and melt things down. If I'd known I'd be out I would have put on my heavy coat, but my boots are on and this jacket is something against the cold.

Eva edged over on her side and the wood rolled, and she rolled with it and turned as she came and sat down on the ground where the couple of round pieces had landed.

Her side hurt her from landing on it, but she was more comfortable on the ground than across the pile.

If I could stand up I would, she thought, but that's the hard part, getting up when you're down. Where she was sitting was all wood chips from the chopping so she wasn't sitting in mud.

If I was closer to the chopping block, she thought, I might be able to pull myself up. Dasn't try on this pile though. Roll the whole thing down on top of me. Emmet'll find my boots is all.

Emmet's the first. Course he never had kids so I don't count up his grandchildren so I go to Donnie. She counted on her fingers and addressed the chopping block. Donnie had Mark and Evelyn. Mark has Cindy, Sarah, Eileen, that's three. Evelyn has James, Gerard, and the girls, Katie and Laura. That's seven. Then Barbara. Barbara had Skip and Andy and Joyce. Skip has the two girls, Jean and Wendy. That makes nine and the two boys Edward and Charles makes eleven. Andy has, let's see, Andy has Karen and Paul, and Florence makes fourteen. Of course, Joyce never married so we go to Lenny. Lenny had Dorothy and Dorothy has Scott, Craig, Debbie, and Lynn. That makes eighteen. Eighteen? Or nineteen? Are there nineteen? Oh, the new baby. Course I missed the new baby back with Andy's wife. That makes nineteen and they haven't decided to call her Christine or Danielle.

Well, that makes all of them, nineteen.

The possum came to the garbage can. Emmet had put a stone on top so the possum couldn't pry off the lid. Eva watched the possum push the garbage can over. The lid clanged off and fell upside down onto the stone and the possum walked into the can.

Better the way we used to do it, Eva thought. Take the garbage out to the woods. Let the critters do over it there where you didn't have to see them or hear them. Now Emmet would have to pick up the mess in the morning.

Wouldn't let her burn the trash anymore either. It was all mixed together in the garbage can. Not like good compost one place and burnables in the barrel and cans to the dump. Everything. Well, he hauled it. Have it his way, but there would be a mess in the morning. She was starting to feel the cold go through her.

The house hadn't taken off in fire yet so maybe it wasn't going to. But it would be cold when they went in when Emmet got home. Maybe she had closed the draft out of habit.

The possum walked out of the garbage can and up the slope to the woods. She'd be having young ones and teaching the young ones how to fend for garbage, Eva thought.

There was Joyce, never married though she was a beauty. So sophisticated when she was in school, belle of the class and being driven everywhere in that young Drew fellow's red car, but building doll houses now, papering the walls, making up the tiny furniture and beds. Eva was starting to feel shivery with the cold going through her.

Night like this, she thought, Alan and I'd go walking. Have on our boots because of the mud and walk down the road looking up at the stars, looking through the night like it couldn't hold us. We'd be holding onto each other and you could hear the brook come crashing down and see up there where the water was white coming over the tree roots where it was chipping the last of the ice and taking it down. The air smelled like maple sap, like you could be swimming in it, warm after the winter. And the bare branches stretched across the sky in places like a net caught full of stars. Alan'd put his arm around me and we'd walk down the road and then we'd walk back, and the feeling'd be big outside and small inside the house and the heat would get us cozy.

But Joyce, she never married. Builds doll houses. And then, when Emmet was born, why we'd carry him out, too. Bundle him up and take him out after supper with Alan carrying him. Then all the kids, and Emmet staying home and the other kids going off.

She hadn't broken anything. She was sure she hadn't broken anything, but Emmet must have got bogged in the mud. He'd get out of the car and he'd walk to Ralph's for the tractor and he'd remember the nights walking after dark down the road with them. His eyes wide and round and the air soft as maple syrup around him. He would remember that. He had never married, moved away like the rest of them. He would help her inside and get the stove going and then the rooms would close and feel small around them.

Now when her mother had died at ninety-three that wasn't mud season. That was July. The temperature stayed near a hundred for three days with the humidity so you felt it on you when you moved. The fields had been cut and lay flat and the trees never stirred except from seven to nine at night when they softly rearranged their leaves and then didn't move until the next night. Then on the fourth day the wind came through and stirred them all around and cleared out the humid air that'd hung there and people took to breathing again. Then she'd gone and tended the garden the rest of the summer and canned sixty quarts of tomatoes off it.

That's when Emmet had been ready for school the next year and the cat brought in the frog and the frog leaped away and Emmet thought it landed in the pot of tomatoes which it just missed, and the cat got it under the stove.

Emmet still would not eat canned tomatoes. Still. If he didn't come soon, she would be pretty cold, too cold to thaw out when the room closed in. He ought to come soon. Even if he had Ralph pull out the car and he walked home, he should be coming soon. If she had the chopping block to climb up on she might be able to. She was getting stiff sitting on the chips. She was getting cold.

I shouldn't stay out this long. I should be inside now. Did I tell you about the great-grandchildren. Yes, you counted. Oh that's right. Nineteen. And about the time Alan died and Emmet was late getting home.

The lights from Emmet's car winged across the field and he made the turn into the driveway and up toward the barn. Eva lifted her head up toward the sky. There was a net of bare branches. Did I tell you about the stars? About the thinnest slice of a moon?

EVERETT

This might be the last day that things are the same, he thought. Everett sat in his chair. He looked out the window over the lawn where the sun smoothed over the petunias. How will this look when I come back, he thought. How different will everything be?

He had never had to stop for gas before anywhere out of town. He drove into the Sunoco and put five dollars of gas into the truck and gave Shep the money. Opened the hood and put in his own oil.

He didn't know if it was his mother or father. He couldn't tell, but this Saturday instead of watering the petunias and watching from the porch to see them straighten up, he took a pair of pajamas, wrapped his toothbrush in them, and his wallet which he never carried around town, just the money, whatever he was going to spend at Sam and George or the five dollars for the gas.

For the first miles on the main road, he drove tipped forward over the steering wheel. He had been out and back before, but he had not been farther than the sheep and lamb auction at the fairgrounds. He went past the fairgrounds. The snow fence blocked his view of the sheep sheds and the midway. Blueweed flowers grew along the fence.

The petunias now would be standing with the water in their stalks, and the cool place of the porch would be dropping off at the edge into heat that came up the steps.

Then he sat back and thought, whatever it is, I'm going forward now, and he let go the hold on the wheel and put his hand on the bottom of it the way he drove in town and thought, it can't be that many years because I'm not that old yet but they've been getting older just the same. Just the same as when they pulled away in the Chevy with the trunk tied down over Mama's rocking chair and the quilts tied on across the roof over the spindle bed frame, he and she looked different than I ever saw them before, this time coming onto them new like this they are going to look different. It's just something I have to prepare myself for. And Aunt Lucille. Now. When she lost her husband and they moved up to her she was thirty-five. She was the baby and Mama was fifty-something.

There was blueweed flower along the edge, and it ran into sand and then sidewalk. He didn't look at the buildings. The buildings were there, small along the road with streets running off and signs, signs. He looked at the gas. He didn't stop. The sidewalk ran into sand and then road weeds. He looked along at the trees and there was highway so he turned onto it. They had told him many years ago sitting at the table where they would go and how to get there. They had planned it on the table, so what he had had to do this morning was to set a place for each of them as if they were still there and follow the route his dad had made with the fork across to his mother's cup and saucer, and then he remembered the route numbers the fork went along and now he knew what route number to look for.

He kept the truck in the right-hand lane. He looked down on the row crops with the barn or the trees in the middle and the tractor stopped in the field and in one field the school bus, parked, and clothes on the clothesline going out from its window. He let the cars go past on the left-hand side. Brush was cut back from the road and the guardrail ran along. And the signs stood up large. He kept the truck along the white line. The truck picked up the road noise and knocked it around between the open windows. The cars passed on the left, and he kept the truck along the white line. And then the route number sign stood up, and he pulled the truck along the white line off the exit and followed the fork to turn right at the exit and left at the center.

Something will tell me, he thought, just like something told me this morning I better come. I just have to watch. I don't know it yet, but something will tell me. He drove on a road that could have been a part of his own main road he hadn't seen yet and after he had driven far enough past the stone walls and the hay fields, then there was on the left, parked, a green truck with a plywood back and roof built on, and Everett slowed and saw the driveway and behind the lilacs, the house with a rope swing coming out of a tree and a woman hanging wash on a clothesline in the back, and he stopped the truck and he thought, so this is it. This is the place they have been since they left with the trunk tied shut, and he turned the truck into the driveway which was gravel with the grass in the center like his own, and he saw the woman stop pulling a sheet up out of the basket, and he saw the Chevy pulled into the carriage shed in the back with freckles of paint off the trunk. And the woman put her hands on her hips.

He drove along the driveway and stopped beside her and said, "Hi, Mama."

"Ain't your mama," she said, pointed, and he saw his mama on the back porch steps with a big girl between her knees on the lower step. His mama was braiding the girl's hair the way he used to see her braid his sister's, and he turned to the woman and said, "Aunt Lucy, then?" though she looked like his mother should have looked.

"You Everett?" the woman said.

"Yes, ma'am."

"Well, come and join the crowd. Your sister's already here and my Calley too. You go on and park in the back."

He drove on the gravel to the end of the carriage shed and stopped the truck and turned it off, and it seemed very quiet to him in the sunlight with the engine off.

He thought maybe a dog would rush up to the side or maybe somebody come from the house, but nobody did so he got out and stretched his arms over his head to give someone the chance, but nobody did so he walked across the gravel to the big girl and his mother on the porch steps.

"Everett," his mother said. "Now we're waiting just on Barnard."

"You all right?" Everett said.

"I'm all right. This is Penelope, your sister Addy's girl. That's Everett, my oldest."

"Dad?" Everett said.

"Yep. He's all right. He and Gabber are down at the stream across the road."

"You all right?"

"I told you yes. And don't tell your daddy about the cake when you see it on the refrigerator because he hasn't seen it yet. We're waiting on Barnard now. Your dad's forgot what day it is now he's at the stream. When Barnard comes we'll have it. You have lunch?"

"No, ma'am."

"You get a plate then. There's beans and potato salad, piece of chicken, you go on in. Penelope you take him."

The girl got up, and he followed her onto the porch and into the kitchen. "Which one is it?" he said. He saw the cake on the refrigerator.

"Fiftieth," she said. "No old folks can remember any dates or years."

He looked at the cake but there was no writing. She gave him a plate and on the counter were the party plates and napkins, gold edged with wedding bells, and, Anniversary, he thought. It's their anniversary. They're both all right, he said. Fiftieth anniversary.

"I go through," his mother was saying to Lucy, "and I see the good times. I don't see any of the bad." He sat on the porch. He saw she was Lucy now and that his mother was his mother. He had them straight and his niece, Penelope. It seemed he was still moving even though he was out of the truck. I will have to buy gasoline, he thought, and then it seemed that the porch was pulling into the back yard in front of the gravel driveway, and Barnard came in with his whole family in the Buick, and Everett went over to the car for when he got out and said, "Well, there you are then. We were waiting for you."

And everyone was out of the car and Lucy was in and out of the house. Nobody sat on the porch steps because the sawhorses were set up with the painted boards across them in the yard, and the women were bringing out the food and setting it.

Everett and Barnard walked around the front to look at Calley's truck with the built-on back, and then here was coming his father across the road coming up with Gabber and a fishing pole and Everett remembered his father carrying him on his shoulders down a path that was beaten earth and with the fishing pole carried along and coming to a rock cut flat across and sitting, watching his father's back and then leaning up against it. He didn't remember where it was. He remembered his father, a lean man, sitting at night with his legs crossed and his elbow crossed onto his knee, thin so that he looked folded together in the short-sleeved shirt. And now he came across the road, Everett saw that he had changed only enough to keep up with his mother and that together they looked just the same as always.

All the young and grown children filled the lawn after lunch, swinging and pushing each other on the rope swing and running around the table until someone finally did knock into it and bump the board off like they said he was going to, so then they brought out the cake and the coffee pot.

Together they cut the cake and Daddy knew very well what day it was and smiled for Lucille who had the camera. Then they ranged the kids by size, and Lucille took their pictures and then they ate the cake.

So that isn't it, Everett thought. It's the anniversary then, and everyone's all right.

"I just always remember the good times," his mother said. The kids stopped running around the table, and the early afternoon stopped for a breath and became late afternoon. Barnard looked at his watch, and Addy pushed kids out of the house to say good-bye, and Calley called her kids from across the driveway, and they pinched frosting from the rest of the cake.

Everett went to the front yard to wave. Calley was in the cab of the truck. He could hear the kids bumping against the plywood in the back, and the truck was on the road with Barnard's Buick in the driveway after it.

And then his mother and his father, Aunt Lucille and Addy were on the porch, and Everett walked across the gravel to his truck.

"Everett," Aunt Lucille called, and he turned with his hand on the door handle, and she took his picture from the porch. He climbed in. His pajamas were on the seat. It's okay, he thought. It wasn't that. I didn't have to stay. It was one of the good times.

"Where can I get gas?" he called as he swung around.

"In the center. Beano's." And he waved, drove past the lilacs.

It was Sunoco and he put in his own oil. "That's the secret," he told the man. "These old vehicles. Doesn't matter the gas, but you keep giving them the same oil. It'll keep them running." He paid for the gas with five dollars from the wallet.

When he came off the highway, it was dusk. He got onto the main road. He began to think of home, of pulling into his own driveway. Then the lights hit across the petunias and the scent they'd been saving came across the air to him in the truck. He turned off the truck and took his pajamas off the seat.

KIM'S LOT

They were banging and moving machinery down
the road in Kim's lot. They had a truck running
down there all the time or coming and going. The flatbed
truck stayed down there all day while the bulldozer ran
over the lot, and pulled out at the end of the day with the
bulldozer on it.

The bulldozer started after the chain saws had felled a
space for it, one month after Virey had sold it to Jeffrey
Smullen at the bank for his son to build a house. She had
sold it all of a sudden after waiting seven years for her own
son to return, to take up the land of his fathers. She had
sold it on a day when to her it seemed more hopeless than
usual to wish for him to come home. She had walked into
Jeffrey Smullen's office on purpose to tell him he could
buy the land, saying, "Yes" instead of, "No, that's Kim's
lot," when Jeffrey said, "How about that piece of land?"
"Yes," she said. "I think so. You can buy it if you buy it
today," knowing she would change her mind, knowing
that the changing of her mind would be one other hurtful
part to remember about Kim.

She had saved Kim's baby teeth in a jewelry box, had
saved them from under his pillow as a reminder that he
had been little once and had needed her, saved them as a
talisman against his forgetting her.

She had heard enough of Alaska in the first days he
was home from the service, and she wouldn't listen to herself when she remembered it was the last frontier. Her
father and her grandfather and his and his had lived here,
if not in this house, in one of the other family houses.

Virey's brother Vince came for coffee with her every Saturday. When Kim was still in the service, Vince said, "He
won't stay." Virey told him what she was going to do, what

she'd done, and Vince said, "He won't stay." She had kept the airplanes set up in his room and known he would want more than just a room when he came home. She had subdivided the piece at the end of the property.

And then Kim was back from the service, not back in the way it would have mattered during the war, but back in the way that people suddenly noticed he'd been gone. What he'd done in the service, Virey saw, was to cut the ties he had to home. He didn't put the airplanes away from his room, and she saw he was only pausing in his race to be somewhere else.

Vince drank the coffee Virey made on Saturday and said, "Virey, he has to be. You have to let him."

"But, it's so far," she said to Vince. "Why so far?"

Then she and Kim were in the kitchen, across from each other at the table.

"What's wrong with it?" Kim said. He was leaning forward toward her. "What's wrong with it?" He had just come in with the tax bills from the mailbox, and he waved them as he spoke. She wouldn't tell him. He should see that she wanted to have him near her with her grandfather's grandfather.

He left the airplanes in his room and the clothes he'd left the first time, and he went out of town, and he went to Alaska.

Virey waited seven years. She thought that seven years was somehow significant in common law. She decided in a moment that she would sell the land to Jeffrey Smullen whose son Jeff was moving back with his family, giving up his city job to come work at the bank with his father. Jeffrey had a picture of them behind his shoulder at his desk when she went in to sell him Kim's lot.

Kim had sent her pictures of his house, his wife, and two little boys. They weren't real to her. She wondered if he had found some boys who looked like him and posed with them. His wife looked as if she couldn't speak. Virey had never heard her say anything.

Virey couldn't see the land from the house. She felt the noise from machinery kick up against the clapboards of her old house. She didn't know what they were building down there. It wouldn't match the style of her house.

A truck went by with planks, and all day after the bulldozing there was hammering. She didn't know how to build a house. Then later in the week the trucks of fill went past.

Virey waited until evening. She waited until the trucks had gone back past her house. No machines were making noise, and she could hear no hammering. Then she walked on the road down past the woods beside her house to the lot she had sold.

The earth that the bulldozer had torn up was powdery brown, and the trees were down. They had the foundation in and had started on the frame. The sticks of framework stabbed at her, but she didn't move. The woods closed in as the dark came down. The powdery earth stood out light-colored.

The stabbing of the sticks was a sharper pain than the ache she had had waiting for Kim to use the land. Virey stood on the road and the dark crept out from the trees. It was easier in the dark to see what the house would be. Fireflies made their light trails across the darkness in front of the house, and Virey turned to walk home.

She thought she'd have a picture taken of herself posing with the new family, not saying anything, posing in front of the lovely front doors it would have with a man and his wife and their children in the sunshine, and send it to Alaska.

FOURTH OF JULY

A nother holiday. Fourth of July. The diner would be packed with people having breakfast on their way somewhere and buying coffees to go. Harold waited until his seat by the back wall was empty, then walked straight down the single aisle and sat in it. The stores would be closed so that in the rush of people moving both ways on the sidewalk he could only look at the windows, not turn in through the glass doors to see the insides. He liked the insides of the stores. Windows were two-dimensional and never showed what was inside, being too loaded with display and nothing of the guts. Inside he never saw the same things that the window displayed.

He usually ate sausage and eggs at the diner, not too early, drank his coffee on the bench beside the tree in front of the diner window, then moved, not too quickly, down one side of Main Street to the firehouse and back the other side. His favorite was the furniture store, but he didn't go in every day. A drugstore you can walk into every morning and browse, but in a furniture store, after a few visits the salespeople wonder what you are doing there and leave you alone or whisper to each other when you come in.

He waited for a special day now and then when he would let himself into the furniture store, a day when he felt either very pleased with himself or very unhappy. Once in a while he walked down along the side of the building where it formed an alley with the florist. There was the side door where trucks unloaded onto the concrete platform. He always let himself stand and watch if they were moving furniture.

Today the sidewalks were so busy that he allowed himself to step into the alley and stand watching the people go by. Already some had settled at the curb with beach chairs to see the parade which would begin at 12:00. Harold moved away from the people and down the alley to sit at the top of the concrete stairs where the trucks unloaded. The rope that hung from the door handle that tied to the iron railing to hold open the door hung right next to him and he began to twirl it and to think that tomorrow he would let himself into the furniture store because today was such a disappointment with all the people everywhere and all the stores closed.

He tugged at the rope, as he would have stamped his foot had he not been sitting, and the door snapped open and tugged once against the rope, and Harold sat and looked at the rope in his hand which went taut to the door that had jerked open behind him.

The noise in the street filled up the alley but behind him, on the end of the rope, Harold could hear the quiet inside of the furniture store. He knew it was dark, could see on the brick wall of the florist's almost, the reflection of the dark where rolled rugs would be standing in the aisle behind the showroom itself. For several minutes Harold held the rope with the weight of the door, then without releasing the hold, not allowing the tautness to move, he gathered his feet and legs under him, pushed a hand against the cement and rose still facing the brick wall. Only after he was standing did he turn to face the door and tug the rope and then he was inside and dropped the rope so that it fell outside and the door shut. The rolled rugs were there in the dim light he saw after a minute's standing still, in the dusk that echoed into the back aisle from the front windows.

He stood in the aisle with the rugs a long time wearing out the wonder before he let himself be curious about the chairs he could see. Then he moved to the backs of the chairs.

Across the lowest part of the windows in red and blue on white banners facing the street, Harold could see

through the white paper the backwards letters, Indepen-
dence Day Sales, July 1–3. He watched the heads go past
the windows and saw the sunshine, which outside he had
not noticed, glinting on eyeglasses and sunglasses and
the frames of baby carriers. It fell through the windows to
make squares on the green carpeting.

Nobody looked at him. Nobody looked at the windows
which outside would be reflected glare. The people kept
going past. Harold moved from the dusky background to
stand by a recliner chair. He watched the window. He sat
on the edge of the chair.

More people stood now at the curb and fewer moved
past the window and the drums pounded in the cool stillness of the furniture store. Shortly Harold could hear the
music and the start of the parade came past the windows
from right to left. He couldn't see the marchers, but the
floats went by, pulled along the tops of the heads in front
of the windows, and he liked the costumes and the scenes.
He especially liked the hats with feathers and the capes.
And when the antique cars went past, he could see the
people in them.

He pushed himself back into the lap of the large chair
and lifted against the arms to raise his feet off the floor,
noiselessly, so that he tipped farther until he was reclining
and had to look along his knees to see out the windows.

His grandfather, on July Fourth, had nailed the spinning fireworks to the tree beside the porch and he sat in
his mother's lap and the aunts and the uncles sat in the
wicker chairs and waited, talking in voices lowered by the
coming dark and watching the first fireflies blink across
the driveway, the first stars prick out through the sky.

He got down off his mother's lap every time he could
and went to the old man on the lawn and said, "Isn't it
time? Isn't it dark enough?" And the old man said, "When
you can't tell the faces on the porch, then it will be dark
enough." And he turned and saw the white faces shining

in the dusk and his mother called him and he climbed again into her lap. "He's not going to fire them yet," and "You stay here so you don't get in the way of one," again.

And, finally, when the voices were almost whispering, almost gone in the darkness, the "Isn't it dark enough?" and his grandfather lit a match against his zipper and held him up to the pinwheel on the tree and pulled him back just in time as the fire chased around and around itself shooting off the sparks, the sparks that Grandpa himself shot off the grinding wheel when he sharpened his axe, but from all sides at once. And somehow he was back on the porch with the skyborne fireworks booming and bursting and shooting colored sparks which arced out and down. And in the real dark and from looking at the bursting light, he could no longer see Grandpa at all on the lawn and filled his eyes with the brightness so that when the last one was done, he closed his eyes and saw them again against his eyelids.

The people were once again moving both directions on the sidewalk and the window squares had skewed to one side on the carpeting and flattened to long points. He watched the street and looked over all the soft chairs and all the hard tables inside the store but did not get up out of the chair. He waited again for the dusk, for it to be dark.

Out in the soft night his hand held the rope for just a minute, then let it go and the door shut and he did not pull the rope again to see if it would open.

THE MAP

I t's a map they sent us," Julie said. "If the power plant explodes, but it's not going to, we'll go to . . ."

"I'm not going."

"Mother, if it does, you'll have to. They won't let you stay here."

"Look at that sun on the lawn. Does it look as though the power plant will explode? Really."

To Julie, the sun on the lawn was dangerous—the poison in the apple. The deadly sweet. She said, "It would be a day exactly like this."

"Then I surely would not go," her mother said. "I would sit in this chair with my knitting on my lap—you make sure I can reach my knitting that's all I ask—and I'll sit here and let radiation creep around me—through me. I don't mind. I hope it's quick."

"But if it's quick, how will I get away fast enough and leave you with your knitting?"

"Oh. Well, I meant quick after you leave, of course. I meant quick so I won't be sitting in the dark waiting for it, imagining things."

"Mother, what worse could you imagine for God's sake than sitting in your chair waiting for the radiation?"

"Worse? I could imagine you stuck on the road in all the traffic or out of gas and no one to help you and everyone out for himself. Traffic jams on all the bridges. You said they're working on them all—down to one-lanes, every highway. Afraid. Everyone afraid they won't make it and others will. You see how people act even on the one-lanes, pushing ahead of others. Can you imagine an emergency? What can I imagine worse? I can imagine when you get there—you and everybody else sitting inside closed houses watching for the winds to push radiation through cracks around the windows. You be sure to open the windows before you leave do you hear me?"

"The windows, yes," Julie said. "And how about me? I feel terrible for leaving you, honey."

"Nothing to do about that. Can't go back. What would you find and you'd be dead doing it. Find what the men in suits with Geiger counters will find. Old woman sitting in chair in front of window. Morning has come again or perhaps several mornings have come—with knitting in her lap, a sweater—almost done. That's it, honey. You can't finish with life."

"But, what if—mother, you've got the windows open— what if something else gets in before the men with suits? What if wild dogs—the ones that run after deer back there? Or people—wild people. What if wild people get in? A man?"

"Are you saying to me that with radiation creeping across the sunlight on the lawn, filling all the spaces between the maple leaves as it comes, slicking the tar on the road and greasing the window ledges I should be worried about . . . I see. You mean tear me apart before it gets here or after?"

"Well, I was thinking before but it could be after just as well. You sure everything that's going to be dead around here is going to be dead at the same time?"

"We could move, you know," her mother said. "Move to Montana."

"Mother, they have buried missile sites in Montana. You wouldn't want to live next to a buried missile site. Anyway, what would I do for work in Montana?"

"Maybe get a job at a buried missile site. Oh, never mind. I was only joking."

Julie said, "Would you like your tea? I'm going to have mine."

"Yes, but close the window here before you go."

Julie didn't go out to turn on the kettle. "I won't leave

you, mother. I'll carry you to the car, you know. I can do it—if I have to knock you out."

"Thank you, dear. Yes, that will be best. Does the car have gas in it? Do you always keep it full?"

"I always keep it pretty full. When it gets to a quarter, I put in gas."

"I think, maybe, when it gets to a half."

"Yes. All right. From now on when it gets to a half. It will be better to have you with me than to feel so bad as I do about leaving you."

"Where will we go? Where will everyone be going?"

"That's why they sent the map. Up to Winsted. That's in the northwest part of the state. They'll be directing traffic."

"They'll be? Who will be? Anybody should be directing traffic's going to take their family and get out of here. Anybody has any sense is not going to stand around directing traffic. I know where Winsted is. Never been there."

"We could go. We could ride out there—see what it looks like. Then it would be familiar. It would be easier."

"I don't want to go there, no."

"Well, we don't have to."

"I mean not at all. You just close the windows when you go, that's all. It might take a little longer. But then, maybe it won't. I don't know. Let me see the map. Oh, yes. I have been there. Once. When you were little. Been through there on the way to somewhere. I don't know. But then the whole center of Winsted, Main Street, was taken out in the flood after that. Taken right out as if it had never been there and all the debris piled down at one end and the mud. Now that was in the rain. That happened when it was raining, you know. Had been raining for days. Dark skies. Dreary so you knew something was coming. We weren't there when it happened, of course. I don't mean that. We just saw pictures in the paper after. But weather like that you expect something to happen is all I mean. It's no surprise that it does."

"Well, Mother, maybe it won't be a day like this that the power plant goes if it goes—which it won't."

"You said it would be exactly like this."

"Well, how would I know what kind of a day it would be? It might be flat down nasty with thunderstorms and tornadoes."

"We don't have tornadoes here, thank God. I wouldn't live here if we had tornadoes."

"Yes, you would, too. You would live here because you were born here. You can say Montana but when it comes right down to it, you'll sit in your chair and say no. I'll take my chances."

"Well, here at least you know what you're in for. Hurricanes, yes, maybe sometimes, but never strong like in Florida and certainly never tornadoes or dust storms that can cut your windows flat into etchings."

"You can say Winsted . . . ," Julie said.

"Let me see the map. Have you looked at the route numbers? There won't be anybody, you know, directing traffic. Everybody in cars going the same way and if someone makes a wrong turn they'll follow. Caterpillars around the rim of the glass, you know. So you'd better learn the routes. You don't want to be looking for the map when you're ready to leave."

"Caterpillars?"

"Caterpillars. You know. What I meant was, you put a caterpillar on the rim of a glass or a bowl or the washtub, say when you were little and would sit in it in the summer in the water. You put a caterpillar on the rim, or he somehow gets there by himself, and he'll follow himself around and around never get off, never, all day all night until he drops off maybe from exhaustion or lack of food or lack of sleep."

"Do they sleep?"

"I don't know if they sleep. But do you know the route numbers for when you leave?"

"I can see them, yes. I'll be fine."

"Thing about maps is, when you come up to an intersection it never looks like it does on the map. It may have a gas station and a pay phone. You can't tell. What you map out just doesn't look like the real thing when you get there. Do you think the phone lines will be working? You could call and let me know you made it."

"I don't think phone lines would be affected. Unless of course they melted. It depends, doesn't it, on how big the explosion is or how far it affects?"

"We're close enough for whatever effects. Across a river doesn't count I don't think. It's the distance. Well, you call then, if you can, if the phone lines haven't melted."

"Well, what if I try to call and I don't know if they're melted and I can't get through? How are you going to feel waiting for me?"

"I'll feel like the phone lines have melted. I'll tell myself as soon as you leave that the phone lines have melted and that I won't hear from you, but you try anyway."

"Well, how about me? What if I hear it ringing so I know the phone lines haven't melted and you don't answer? How will I feel knowing I left you sitting there?"

"Well, I can't answer the phone anyway unless you move it in here before you go."

"Yes, so why should I ring it?"

"Julie. Move it in here before you go or buy another phone and we'll leave it plugged in here. Is it too much to ask to phone me? I'll wait for the phone call and I won't hear the radiation."

"I'll buy a phone. All right. I'll buy a phone and keep gas in the car. You won't hear the radiation. The windows are shut."

"Will I hear the sirens? How long will they keep on with the sirens?"

"Until someone turns them off, I guess. They're automatic, aren't they?"

"Maybe they shut off automatically, then. They might do that. After a few hours. Or they might just keep on. Maybe I won't hear the phone then. I'll think it's the sirens. Or I'll keep hearing it and pick up and it won't have rung. You won't be there."

"I don't have to call."

"You call, yes. But if I don't answer, it might be the sirens. Yes, that's it. You call, but if I don't answer, it's the sirens. That's all. You fold the map and put it in the glove compartment is what you ought to do. So you don't have to look for it."

Julie went out to turn on the teakettle. The cups were already on the tray. Sunlight fell past the window onto the heated summer grass.

GRAVES OF THE DAUGHTERS

Now Ella is gone. Now Carlotta is gone. Aurelia and Howard ride one on each side of the car, Aurelia sunken toward the right-hand door and Howard toward the left with the steering wheel in front of him.

When Aurelia wants to see where the car is going she tilts her head toward the right where the dashboard slopes down to the windshield and she can see over it. When she doesn't care where the car is going she looks at the dashboard, the glove compartment in front of her, and the Mercury insignia.

When Howard wants to see where the car is going he stiffens his muscles and looks through the steering wheel and over the dash. He holds onto the bottom of the steering wheel to push against. He can see above the road without tensing, but he cannot see the road. When he tilts his head to the left to look above the slope of the dash toward the windshield, he steers left. "Am I clear?" he says to Aurelia on the right-hand side.

When they get into the car, Aurelia and Howard drive to the cemetery. They get out of the car to look at the graves of their daughters, Ella and Carlotta. "Ella had such a lovely voice," Aurelia says. "Always singing. Always cheerful."

Howard says, "And Carlotta. Remember when she thought she could fly and skinned her knees flying out of the apple tree?"

Aurelia is in the habit of leaning against the car door and tilting her head. Out of the car, she tilts suddenly against Howard. She has just said, "Such beautiful girls," and Howard is about to say, "They took after you," when Aurelia leans suddenly against him, and he loses his balance. They fall down on the soft spring earth as they had been down on the grass the spring they had first known each other and married so suddenly and could chase around on the tough grass of the hayfield and catch each other.

On the ground with Aurelia against him, Howard said, "Remember spring of '26?"

"I remember," she said, and she remembered the wind blowing the fall's leavings across the spring hayfield where the grasses bent down, wide and tough. That was many years before they needed the girls, before they had thought to be surprised that in all the chasing and catching she never conceived. She was surprised that she remembered with her body the hot fast urgency of their need to be together.

Today in the cemetery, it wasn't windy. Last year's leaves stayed in the long grasses. They had been coming to the cemetery for eighteen years this spring. This day reminded her also of the day they had come and chosen their daughters. She didn't know what birds they were, but some birds in the cedar trees were making noise. "It was a day like this," she was thinking, "that we came here and chose them from the names and the stones."

"It's not your real sister," Aurelia had told her friend Mary Jean when they were kids and Mary Jean's parents had adopted a four-year-old girl and cut off her braids and kept them in tissue paper in a box in the vanity.

Lying on the still grass, Aurelia saw that she had been wrong. "It is your real sister," she called silently to Mary Jean wherever she was, "You were right," and took Howard's hand and told him, "It is too bad that Carlotta's hair was so unruly that we had to cut off her braids and keep them."

"But it was so beautiful short, with the waves in it."

The sun was warm, but it brought out the dampness of the ground beneath them. Howard was still, and he was looking into the sky. Aurelia turned herself off his legs and rested beside him another minute.

"We certainly are fortunate—such wonderful girls," he said before he moved to get up.

She had not hurt him, and he had not hurt her. They moved carefully on the grass. First they sat. Then they moved, sitting and pushing with their arms to reach the stone that had Ella's name. Howard pushed his right foot down as on a gas pedal and clutched an invisible steering wheel and Aurelia leaned right and called, "All clear." They pulled themselves to the stone and held on and lifted each other up. Aurelia thought she would feel the bruises tomorrow. They stood in front of the stones.

"They took after you," Howard said then.

They helped each other to the car. The sun came down on the grasses and drew the dampness from the ground where they'd been. It was warm in the car. Howard started the engine. Aurelia tilted toward the right-hand door. Howard tilted toward his own door and turned the car in a wide circle to the left.

ARROWHEADS

From standing halfway up the mound of earth, in the rain, with the footprints he had made settled into the rain in the mound, Arnold looked up under his hat to watch the pickup pull off the road and stop next to his. He put his head down so the other fellow wouldn't see him looking. "Damn," he said, slammed the word down with the rain into the mound of earth. Rain clamored on the metal parts of the trucks and ran to the ground and Arnold looked under his hat brim. Cars with their lights on, though it was morning, went past on the road beyond the trucks. Nobody he knew. Young fellow. No hat.

Arnold looked down again at the mound he was working over.

"Morning," he said under the hat to the fellow at the foot of the mound.

"Morning," fellow said. "Mind if I come up?"

Arnold didn't move. "Help yourself."

Fellow walked around the edge of the mound outside the puddles, and then crossed and started up near Arnold. His boots sank into the mound and he turned himself sideways to go up. "Used to have a sandpile," he said, "when we were kids, out by the house. Spend all day there digging tunnels." He stooped and picked up something. Rain hit his head and his back.

"What you got?" Arnold said.

"Oh, nothing. Piece of rock." Fellow rubbed it with his thumb, put it in his pocket.

"You see when they were digging this?" Arnold said. "Took a while to take down trees."

Fellow said, "Naw. Don't live around here."

"Putting back a road," Arnold said. "Where you from?"

"Upstate."

"Yeah? What brings you down here?"

"Well, I saw your truck, and I saw you on the pile..."

Arnold said, "I know every place around here. Yup. Have looked in 'em all." Arnold watched the rain dig fingers into the mound, leave pits that the next fingers covered.

"Any luck?" fellow said.

"Well...luck? No. I always feel I'm close, though. I seem to feel I'm close. Like this mound here. I been watching them push this around, saying 'When they get out of the way one day, the first day they're out of the way, you get yourself over...' "

Fellow said, "Too bad it had to rain."

"Too bad?" Arnold jabbed a finger next to a piece of flint. "Brings 'em right to the top, rain does. You been doing this long?"

The back of the fellow's shirt was wet and rain made an arc down from his waistband. "What is it you're looking for?" he asked.

Arnold leaned away from the mound to look at the fellow. "You didn't stop to look for arrowheads? What we been talking about?"

"Stopped because I saw your truck and this nice fine pile of dirt. You been doing this long?"

"All my life and I'm sixty-five."

Arnold didn't believe him. That fellow had an arrowhead in his pocket. Picked it up first thing. On the mound he'd been watching. Walked up and put it in his pocket.

"Get to the point I say I'll give it up," Arnold said. "I'm going to stop thinking arrowheads and give it up and then comes a rainy day like this and a mound I been noticing and right away I'm out here. Pull in the truck and say if I don't find something in an hour...and at eleven still saying if I don't find something, then, by noon."

Arnold leaned over the mound. "Close my eyes I see earth...pebbles."

Fellow said, "You think it covers up some, too?"

"Naw," Arnold said. "Not likely. See this? See how this

stone is setting with the dirt washed out around? You see? The rain is going to do that 'cause the soil is softer. It can wash away the grains. Ain't going to move the stone much or dig it in. Sometimes make a little pedestal like that." Arnold pointed and the fellow leaned over. "There'll be the arrowhead setting on it. I know fellows have found 'em like that. Have to be willing to still yourself is what it is. Still yourself and take it if it's coming to you. Sometimes when I'm doing this I forget who I am. I surprise myself, you see. Sometimes I forget and think I'm an Indian and can know about storms and spirits and . . ."

Arnold heard himself talking out loud and, "Well, you know, you do this long enough you can get like that," he said. He moved sideways a distance and the rain came down between them.

Arnold was thinking, Fellow's not even looking for arrowheads. Has one in his pocket. You watch. He won't show me, no. Drive in from nowhere. Mound I been watching and you'll see, snatch it away.

Arnold worked his back around to the fellow and the fellow moved in the boot marks that were sinking with rain back into the mound.

"You got somewheres you said you have to get, have you?" Rain dropped his words into the mound and Arnold let them fall dropping into sand and gullies and running, some of them, to the bottom of the mound into puddles that reflected grey dull sky. Rain came down between them, beat the earth from around the stones.

Arnold stayed leaned over and the fellow stood up in the rain and pulled the flint out of his pocket. "Is this something, then, you think?"

He held it on his palm and rain hit it and Arnold looked. It was a beauty. Nary nicked even, tell where the shaft . . . "Yeah," Arnold said. "Yeah, that's something, I guess." From his mound, that he would have found if the fellow hadn't stopped, hadn't pulled over.

The fellow leaned to the mound and placed the arrowhead on the earth. Rain touched it and moved it by a fraction to the side and set it in the mound, began to settle dirt around it.

"That's a beauty," Arnold said. He looked at the arrowhead that stuck out from the mound where the rain glazed it and his tongue stuck in his mouth and he couldn't look at the fellow.

Rain beat the earth between them, easing the boot marks and picking out stones.

Fellow said, "Guess I'd better leave it then. You take it. That's for you. You been looking all along for this one."

Arnold looked at the fellow. Fellow was wet with the rain, looking down at the arrowhead and then back at his pickup.

"Naw," Arnold said. From some great distance, he heard his voice. "That's yours. You take it."

"You would have found it, hadn't been for me," the fellow said, turned, moved down the mound and his boots made marks that had always been there.

"I mean it," Arnold called after him. He followed him to the bottom, near the puddles.

Fellow went straight to the truck, waved through the windshield at him, started the wipers and Arnold waved, kept his back to the mound.

When the truck was on the road, Arnold climbed into his truck and slammed the door. His wet clothes chilled him against the seat and he stared at the mound. Waves of rain slammed across the windshield and Arnold glared at them and started the truck, slammed off the water with the wipers and pulled out.

It was coming on dark—evening—and the rain had stopped and hung above the mound between the earth and sky in spirits, blew across Arnold's back and chilled wet places on his clothes. He was afraid to stand straight and feel how stiff he was. Bowed, he went to the truck and pulled on the lights and went back to the mound to start again at the bottom.

"Damn," he slammed into the soil. I know it was this side because I could see his truck right . . . his truck was right, and mine was . . . I was halfway . . . You'd have to say halfway.

LIDA ROSE

Mrs. Fisher had a picture of her first husband on her desk and her second husband next to him. The first husband wore a soldier's uniform. The second husband had on a suit and was standing on a lawn.

Her name had always been Fisher. Her mail came to Lida or to Mrs. Earnest. At 9:20 she watched for Henry Walkley to come in his battered car with U.S. Mail and two yellow lights on the top. When she saw him, she started to her mailbox and got there just after he left. Henry knew if he had a package, she would come down, and waited for her. Today there was no package. He drove on, and Mrs. Fisher opened her mailbox.

Letter from her sister, Dutch bulbs flyer, YOU HAVE WON FLORIDA VACATION STOP. She walked to the house and sat on the porch. Her sister was twelve years younger than she, only seventy-four, and she complained in every one of her letters about one ailment or another. Poison ivy is bad, her sister wrote, but not as bad as the shingles I had last year.

Mrs. Fisher looked up from the letter.

A truck banged to a stop in the road by her mailbox. Mrs. Fisher stood up. A man leaped down from the cab, went around and lifted the hood. Steam came banging out, and he leaped backwards, bounded up the lawn to her and cleared the steps to the porch.

"Good morning," he said. "Excuse me, but I think I'm out of water. Well, not out, but would you have a jug or a watering can or something that I could use to fill the radiator?"

"Good morning. What's the matter with your truck?"

"Well, I don't think the hose is gone. But it leaks water. Radiator is low on water. Turns the rest to steam."

"Don't you think you ought to sit down for a minute? You shouldn't open that radiator hot like that and pour down cold water. Nope. You sit down. I'll get you a nice drink of cold tea. Then we'll fix the truck."

"A nice... I'm supposed to be at work right now. Supposed to already be there."

"Don't think you're going anywhere in a truck with no water. Don't think you better open that radiator cap. Burn your arm. You sit right on the steps there in the shade, and I'll bring cold tea."

"Use your phone?"

"Oh, why certainly." She held the screen door for him. "Right there on the desk."

She went past it to the kitchen. When she came back with the tea, he was hanging up the phone. He held the screen door, and they went out to the porch.

"I see you were looking at the pictures of my husbands," she said.

"Why, uh... yes. Good-looking men, I was thinking."

"Well, you sit down. Well, when we were kids, we were all sisters. All six of us. And we all married in turn except me. I was the oldest. My youngest sister died first. Childbirth. We never ever saw her again after she married and moved west.

"That man, my first husband, was handsome. He was flamboyant, what you'd call, a hero-looking man I met at a home social when he was visiting with a buddy. Well, he swirled me around for one week and then left for the service. But he came back, swirled through again on leave and just on his own momentum, so to speak, swirled both of us out to Albany.

"Well, I wrote to my mother, described the wedding service, and never saw him again. Worked for a tailor who owned the rent. At night I made doll clothes for the children of the customers. Then I had to write to my mother he was dead with honors. Went on my own tailoring. Moved to a better rent. You married?"

"Me? Uh . . . no. I'm not married."

"Well, you don't have to be in a rush to get married. Married isn't everything. I think if you're young and the . . ."

"Excuse me. You had a second husband?"

"Oh. Well, my given name was Rose, you see. But then when that barbershop singing was getting popular with 'Lida Rose' I thought I'd just change it to Lida, and I count that for the good fortune of my second husband. He was a song-lover himself and he just couldn't get over my name being Lida Rose like the song of course."

"And he . . . ?"

"Died. Yep. He died before I moved here ten years ago. Let me fill your glass." She opened the screen door.

The young man was back at the truck leaning under the hood. She set the glasses on the porch rail and crossed the lawn.

"Has it cooled down, do you think?"

"If I had a rag or a potholder."

"I can get you one." She crossed the lawn to the house, back to the road.

He unscrewed the radiator cap. "I think it's all right to pour in water if you have a . . ."

"Oh, that walking," Mrs. Fisher said. She had the back of her wrist against her forehead. "Has made me just a little dizzy." She put her other hand against the fender of the truck.

The young man was looking at her. She started to sink against the fender, ready to crumple, but he put his arm around her, scooped his other arm under her knees and lifted her up. She leaned her head against his shoulder, and he carried her across the lawn to the porch. "Shall I . . . ?"

"If I could just sit in the chair." He stepped onto the porch and set her into the porch chair, moved his arm from behind her head.

"Oh, I don't know what . . . I felt so dizzy for a moment. Thank you."

"Should I get you . . . here. Sip this tea," he said and brought a glass from the railing.

"Yes. Thank you. I really. . ."

He drank the other glass of tea. "Feel a little better?"

"Oh, yes. Much."

"About that watering can."

"Oh, yes. You go around the side of the house and you will see the hose and the watering can. Just unscrew the sprinkler."

The young man filled the radiator and returned the watering can. He came to the porch. "Well, thank you, then. Do you feel all right?"

"Oh, yes. I'm fine now. You stop again sometime."

He started the truck and waved, and the truck pulled away from the mailbox. Mrs. Fisher looked down at the letter from her sister.

Her sister had nothing to write about. Mrs. Fisher moved in to her desk and turned toward the wall the pictures of the two men she had never met.

Dear Josie,

I've just met the most charming man in the most alarming way. I fainted on the front lawn trying to help fix his truck in the heat and he carried me in to bed.

Birthday at Savin Rock

Manda had the cat mask over her face. She was thinking of birthdays at home. She was thinking of Savin Rock Amusement Park that smelled like cotton candy after the car went under the tunnel from west, Daddy said, to east, and that had tarred walks cracked where tree roots had turned them up and little puddles from the night before drying in sunshine.

The cat mask covered her face down to her mouth and Manda placed a kitchen chair next to the outside door.

Ned was out in his own car delivering mail. He felt it an insult to a man of forty-two who was the postmaster. He didn't wait to put up all the mail, left early with what was already done, kept the car as far away as he could from bushes, opened mailboxes, and tossed mail to the back. He had been a newspaper boy.

He counted the large box he would have to deliver to Manda Everly at the elderly housing as halfway. The package was not heavy but it wouldn't fit through the window of the car. He could leave it on the porch or walk up and ring. After that he would drive a little faster, maybe skip some mailboxes and be back in his office before the heat.

Ned left the car door open, stepped onto the porch of the apartment holding the large package, and pushed the button under the label, H Manda Everly.

He looked through the gap he had just stepped through, where the steps came between the porch railings, at the car with the door slung open, bright in the sun. Behind him the apartment door swung open and tipped him inside. He tripped on the doorsill and, holding onto the package, caught one shoulder against the door jamb and saw, over his shoulder, what he thought was a cat. He turned to tip into the room and the cat closed the door and pushed a kitchen chair against the backs of his knees and he sat, hard, on the chair seat. It was a cat, he saw, with the body of Manda Everly, and the cat, while his hands were full of package, tied him with two jump ropes to the chair. He sat holding the package in front of him keeping it from touching his lap as she tied the ropes under the package, around his chest and arms, and behind the chair.

The cat came around in front of him. "What is this?" he said.

"It's my birthday." The cat sat back down in the chair facing the door. "Down at the Club 70—you know about that? Where they serve lunch for the elderly?—They're going to have a birthday cake for me and a special place at the head of the table and birthday cards that say life begins at 80, and I'm not going. I am not."

"Oh," Ned told her. Below the elbows, his arms were free to lift or lower the package. "Happy birthday."

"I knew you'd say that," the cat said. "You can watch me decorate. I already made the cake."

"I didn't bring a present," Ned said.

"But, yes you did. I knew you would."

Ned held the package.

"I mailed it to me."

"Do you know what's in it?"

She nodded.

"But it won't be a surprise."

"You're surprised, aren't you? And I've had my surprise, too, with you walking in instead of Jamie Pearson. Where's he today?"

"Called in. Wife's about to have their baby and he drove her to the hospital."

"You'll have to hold that a little longer." She climbed onto the step stool and taped an end of crepe paper to the corner of the bookcase. "Until I put on the party cloth." She climbed down and went up again with a Japanese paper lantern. She hung seven lanterns from the ceiling. "I always wanted to have a paper birthday cloth, says happy birthday around the edge," she said.

Through the mask she looked at him while she unfolded the paper tablecloth.

"You're early," she said. "I was just trying out the mask." She spread the cloth over the table. "I wanted to decorate so I could wait. Don't you remember what it's like to wait for your birthday to finally come?"

Ned held the package above his lap. His arms were getting tired, but he didn't set it down.

"Plastic forks I like," she said and went around the room divider to get them and brought out the cake. "You do like cake," she said through the mask.

She took the package from him and set it onto the table with the cake. Ned let his arms down to his lap. Now that they were free of the package it seemed impossible to him that he had let her tie him to the chair. He reached around behind him and felt the plastic handles of the jump ropes.

"That baby's going to be born on my birthday and when I leave she can have it. But there isn't any more Savin Rock. She's going to have to make her own."

Manda sat in a chair next to the table.

"Cotton candy," she said, "it smelled like. You ever go there?"

"I think we may have—a couple of times—when we were kids—saltwater taffy?"

"Saltwater taffy is right, young man. Right next to the ocean and when we'd be almost there mother would say, 'Smell the ocean', and you could. It was clean then and smelled tangy like drops of salt fog on your skin. Sunlight at the ocean dropped straight down the fronts of white houses until we got there." Manda folded her paws in her lap. "Read an article that they've closed up Savin Rock. I thought they had done it a long time ago."

She looked at Ned who placed his hands across his knees where they would just reach against the ropes.

"I thought of giving you a birthday hat, but I thought you were going to be Jamie Pearson. I don't know. Maybe you'd like one. We could look in the closet."

Ned put out his arms to show her that he was tied across his chest to a chair.

"Bring it with you." She smiled and crossed to the closet and opened the door. Coats and dresses hung from the clothes pole. Umbrellas and handbags hung from hooks on the door. "Hats are with the shoes," she said and pointed to a jumble on the floor.

Ned put his hands under the seat of the chair, lifted himself with it and, bent forward, crossed to the closet.

"How are you going to reach them?" Manda said. She turned the cat face to the jumble on the floor and back to him. "I won't untie you yet. Not yet. Can you tip to the side?"

Ned brought the chair under him to the door jamb and tipped sideways against the coats against the cold winter smell of them and caught himself against them with his hands and worked back onto the chair. "Nope," he said. "I don't think so." He moved the chair out of the doorway.

The cat sat down in the doorway and moved her paws through the jumble of shoes and hats and held up a battered red felt. "Cowboy hat," she said. "What you need."

Ned ducked his head forward to put it on. He backed the chair from the closet door.

"Have the six-guns here, too, you want 'em."

Ned waited. Manda moved a clutter of winter boots and a belt buckle hit the door jamb. She pulled on it and two holsters, one with a toy six-gun, followed the buckle out of the pile and onto her lap.

"There," she said. "You don't need the other one." She handed the belt and holsters to Ned. Ned slid out the six-gun and checked it and slid it back in. He kept the holsters and belt across his lap and moved the chair again. He held his arms out to Manda and she pulled herself up and closed the closet door.

"You bring that chair to the table now. I made a marble cake with frosting. We are not going to sing happy birthday. You don't mind?"

"I hate happy birthday," Ned said and took the six-gun out of the holster and shot it at the ceiling. Plow. Plow. Plow. Plow. He tossed it to his other hand. Plow, plow.

He put the gun into the holster and moved the chair to the table. "When are you going to open the present I brought? I think you'll like it."

"After the cake," she said. "Do you like ice cream?"

"Yes," Ned said. "Yes. If it's chocolate."

"It's vanilla, chocolate, and strawberry."

"I only like the chocolate."

"All right, chocolate. I was thinking just this morning that at five years old you eat every bit of sweet and want more. Then when you're twenty, you buy your own sweets and you finish them when you have them."

She cut two pieces of cake and put them onto plates. She dug ice cream from the box and put chocolate on Ned's cake. She put vanilla and strawberry on hers.

"But at forty you can afford whatever sweets you want." She slid a plate across to Ned and sat down at the table. "And you see, biting into a Parisian that you've bought yourself at the bakery, that you might not finish it. So you take the sweetest bites. The bites you want."

She pressed her plastic fork into the ice cream. "At forty, for the first time, you see that you may not finish life. So," she slipped the ice cream into her mouth under the mask and waved the fork at him, "you eat just the chocolate if that's what you want."

Ned picked up the plastic fork and pressed it into his cake. "Are you going to leave some of your cake, then?"

"No. I'm eating every bit of it."

"And then will you open your package?"

"I can't wait to see what's in it." Manda wiped the kitten whiskers with her napkin. "Will you have another piece?" she said.

"I think you should open your present, thank you."

Manda moved the dishes from the table and Ned moved his chair back.

"You don't ever want to cut the strings or ribbons," Manda told him. The mask made her move her head in small jerks, and she looked like a kitten playing with the package. "Tape is all right, though." She used the cake knife to slit the tape and left frosting and crumbs on the edges of the box she opened.

"Oh, how nice." She lifted out a birthday gift with ribbons.

Plow. Plow. Plow. Ned shot at the ceiling. "Don't cut the ribbons," he said. He moved his legs, and the chair tied to his back rocked like a horse, and he moved his legs some more. Plow. Plow. Good and louder.

Manda slipped the ribbon off the corner of the package and tore off the paper. "I always wanted to do that," she said. The kitten mask went up to Ned and down to the package. "But at my house we saved paper."

She lifted the lid off the box and Ned leaned forward, ready to fire. Inside the box was a birthday gift wrapped in paper and ribbon. She held it up.

"It's a trick," she said. "What's in here is very tiny."

Ned sat back and bucked the chair. The legs hit the floor and he bucked it again. Manda unwrapped four more birthday gifts from inside boxes and Ned bucked the chair to the closet and back. Plow. Plow. Plow. The hooves of the horse beat loud, sharp clods of dirt out of the wooden floor and Manda opened the last gift and held it up to show him.

Plow. Plow. The horse bucked him almost off. His shots were going wild.

The kitten held up a locket, and he aimed at it, but the horse bucked and the bullet went into the closet door. Plow. And Manda snatched the locket back.

Outside the door was a tumbling and scurry on the porch, and someone knocked loudly on the door.

Ned held onto the horse and the gun. Manda ran around the table and looked out the side window. "Your car has the door open," she said. "And Club 70 is on the porch with a cake."

"Surrounded," Ned shouted and ducked his head to reach it with the flat of his hand and push the hat down hard.

Outside he could see the posse and the horses. He could feel them closing in. "Ain't none of us going to get out of this alive," he shouted.

WOODLOT

The state trooper's car pulled up and stopped on the road. Asel watched from up the slope, looked down over the stumps and the brush tops of the trees he had cut to the road where his station wagon was pulled over with the trailer behind it loaded with wood cut to stove length.

When the trooper climbed out and looked up the slope at him, Asel cut the engine on the chain saw, rested the saw against his thigh, held it with both the handles, but with the engine cut off to hear the trooper if he was going to say something.

The trooper started climbing past the stumps where Asel had cut the trees off—not large trees, good size that he'd only have to split once if he had to split them at all—and past the brush tops that Asel had pulled to one side so there was a clear path down the slope.

The trooper climbed as high as Asel and moved a step uphill and came to where Asel was standing with the chain saw against his leg. Asel turned his whole body as the trooper came up to the side and one step above him, turned his body toward the trooper so he was no longer facing the road.

And then he heard the sound on the road that would be George Bates pulling his truck over behind where the trooper had parked, and he turned with a quick motion of his head only, holding his shoulders and his body squared toward the trooper, turning his head toward the road where Bates had just climbed out of and slammed the door of the truck.

Then he turned his attention toward the trooper and waited for Bates to come up to both of them on the slope if he was coming.

The trooper said, "Well, looks like you've got a nice trailer load of firewood there."

"Yup," Asel said. He held the chain saw in front of his body with both hands.

"Looks like you've been doing some cutting here." The trooper indicated with his head the stumps and the brush tops. He didn't nod toward the chain saw Asel was holding. He waited for Asel to say something, but Asel held the saw and kept quiet.

He was partly watching, though he didn't cut his eyes around, for Bates to climb up the slope to them. He thought it was past time that if Bates was going to climb up to them, he would have reached them.

Asel didn't say anything. The trooper said, "I'd make a guess, if I had to, that that load of firewood in your possession on the back of that trailer hitched to your car, came from this woodlot."

Asel stood with the chain saw and turned his head to see where Bates had gone if he hadn't climbed up here with them. Bates was down on the road with his foot on the bumper of his truck. Asel saw that he had lighted a pipe and was smoking. He turned back to the trooper.

"Well?" The trooper waited, and Asel said nothing.

"Well, what do you say? Did you cut that wood?"

"Yup," Asel said. "No law against cutting firewood I know of."

"Nope. No law against cutting firewood I know of either as long as it's on your own property. You own this property?"

"Nope," Asel said. "But I know the man that does."

"Yes? And he asked you to cut it? Trailer it off, maybe? Get it out of his way so he wouldn't have to cut it? Wouldn't have to burn it in his stove?" The trooper paused and watched him. Asel waited. "You recognize the man down there his foot against the bumper?"

"Yup. He's the one." Asel did not look down to the road.

"He tells me he never gave anyone permission to cut up here. Came and got me especially to tell me that no one had permission to cut up here."

"You telling me I have to stop?"

"Yes, I'm telling you you have to stop."

Asel looked at the trooper, looked at Bates with his foot against the front bumper of his truck where it was parked behind the state trooper's car behind Asel's trailer on the road. Bates and the vehicles looked shortened by distance and by the angle.

"You mean you can stop me from cutting this wood."

"Yes, we can stop you. Course we can stop you. Don't have permission to cut wood on somebody's land, you can't just go and cut. Course we're going to stop you."

"All right, then." Asel didn't look at him again. He pushed the chain saw from in front of him and held it in his left hand, crossed a few feet downhill of where the trooper was standing, picked up his axe from where he'd leaned it against a stump, and carried it in his right hand, and walked down the slope he'd cleared.

He went down carefully. It was a steep slope, too steep for Bates to get his woods tractor up and haul the wood down if he cut it. Asel went down carefully in his stiff boots between the stumps and the brush to the road.

He didn't look at Bates as he came down. He put the trooper's car between them as he went to the trailer and set in the axe and wedged the chain saw where it wouldn't tip. He swung the can of oil-and-gas mix up onto the load of wood and wedged it in, too, went around the edge of the trailer to the driver's side of the car and opened the door and got in.

The trooper was outside the door. Asel wasn't angry yet. He hadn't said anything against Bates yet, though there was a woodlot Bates wasn't using that he was kicking him off.

"What about the load?" the trooper said across the open

door. Asel hadn't closed it yet. He looked over the top edge of the door where the trooper was standing.

"The load?"

"The trailer load of wood?"

Asel had his hand wrapped around the windowsill of the door where he was going to slam it closed and hold his elbow on it. "What about the trailer load of wood?" Asel said.

"Well, you've got to return it. It isn't yours."

"I've got to what?"

"You've got to return it to the owner. It doesn't belong to you."

"What are you telling me?"

"You can't drive out of here with that trailer load of wood. You've got to return what you've taken off this man's property to the rightful owner of it. Bates said he wouldn't press charges against you. But you still can't steal his wood."

"This wood? On the trailer? That I done already cut?"

"That's right. It doesn't belong to you. It belongs to George Bates."

Asel kept his hand wrapped around the windowsill and looked over the top edge of the door where the trooper was standing.

"I can't let you drive out of here until you've unloaded the wood," the trooper said one last time.

"Until I've... I cut that wood. I spent all day cutting that wood down, loading it onto the trailer, cutting another one to make a load. That's not his. That cutting, hauling is mine. Hauled it down by hand. I don't just give that away, a whole day of work."

Now he was starting. At first the trooper could have been making up that he wouldn't let him pull out, but now he saw that he meant it. Asel pulled himself out of the car by his hand on the windowsill and took hold of the door frame on either side of the empty window space and looked over the top of the door at the trooper standing outside the door on the road.

"You say what?"

The trooper spoke to him now as if he were hard of hearing. "I say George Bates won't press charges if you're reasonable and return his property to him. It's his wood."

Asel worked up to spit. Then he spat. He held the door frame. He wouldn't look back at the load on the trailer behind him. Then he wouldn't look at the trooper outside his car door. He screwed his eyebrows down over his eyes and he worked his chin forward of his upper teeth. Then he worked up to spit. He spat into the road over his stiff left arm. Then he didn't look up at the slope either. He pushed off the door frame where he'd been holding, and he sat in the driver's seat and grasped the steering wheel.

His chin and bottom jaw were stuck up, and he worked his lips around to accommodate them. He looked straight ahead through the windshield.

"Let 'im take 'em," he said. "But not the saw or the axe. Them's mine."

The trooper shifted in the road, let his shoulders sag "You're going to have to unload the trailer," he said.

"Not me."

"Yes, you. Bates has legal right to press charges against you. Says he won't do that, though, if you return his stolen property. You'll have to unload the trailer."

Asel got out of the car again and walked stiffly to the back of the trailer. He started cursing then. "Man's not using the lot." He cursed. "'Nother man needs the wood, does all the work." He cursed. He put the chain saw and the gas can and the axe down from the back of the trailer onto the edge of the road by the back tire. He picked up a chunk and heaved it without looking onto the slope at the side of the road. Heaved the next chunk onto it. "Waits till the wood is cut and hauled to call in the troopers." He cursed.

"Just a minute." The trooper was beside him, at the back of the trailer. Asel placed his hands onto the chunks on the trailer, his arms bunched up at the shoulders, and looked down at the cut wood in front of him. He scrunched his eyebrows down over his eyes, pushed his chin down onto his chest and waited, breathing heavily from throwing the wood and from cursing.

George Bates' truck started and pulled up outside the trailer on the road.

"Just a minute," the trooper said. "The man says since his truck is right here you can take the wood off'n the trailer, put it in the back of the truck." Asel didn't look over. He cursed quiet and steady, his chin pressed into his chest, his voice hitting into the wood on the trailer.

He took another chunk off the trailer. His arms jolted the chunk off the pile and threw it from him onto the others where the slope met the road.

"Ain't going to do that," Asel said, and his arms jolted another one off, and it hit the first ones.

Bates' truck stayed alongside the trailer, and Asel didn't look at it, and he knew when the trooper had gone from beside him and was around talking to George Bates in the truck, and his arms jolted the next chunk off and threw it onto the pile he was building alongside the road, up from the road if he could, so they wouldn't be too close or roll back down.

He knew when the trooper left the other side of the truck and climbed into the state police car, and his shoulders bunched and his arms jolted the wood from the trailer and flung it onto the pile, and he cursed onto the wood, and then, after a long time of jolting, he cursed onto the empty boards of the trailer. Asel swung the axe and then the gas can and then the chain saw onto the bare boards of the trailer and stomped between the trailer and Bates' truck where it was parked, with the engine running, in the road and got into the driver's seat and crashed the door shut between him and the road and started the car. He pulled out from Bates' truck and the state trooper's car, and he didn't look in the rear view mirror.

He worked up to spit, and he spat through the open window onto the road, and he didn't look in the mirror.

MRS. BELDEN

Things disappeared into that house: the cat, groceries, Mrs. Belden herself. When Mr. Belden lived there, he opened the door to let the cat out, leaned way out onto his walking stick or walked out into the yard his wholeself and poked the stick around the new spring flowers or the rustler leaves. But he stopped coming out and the mail carrier told Essie, next house down, that Mrs. Belden told him Mr. Belden had left and she had no forwarding address and he could just leave the mail for him right there same's he always had.

And Essie said, "Elton has turned around and left her. 'S younger than she is by a good few years and he saw that the grass was greener and left her for a younger woman," and took her mail inside to think about that. "But in my opinion, if you ask me, she'll make out better anyway, since it's her family house. And now she won't have an old man to take care of all her days," she told Rake when she put down the lunch plates on the table, and standing above the table, standing on tiptoe, tried to see above the hedge what was going on next door.

"Sit down, for petesake. How can I eat?" When the hedge plants were new she could still see right into the yard same as always. But over the years as they grew up, she took to looking down over the hedge by tipping her chin up and sighting down her nose. She could no longer see over them at all but she still stood on tiptoe, tipped her chin up and sighted out the window as if she could see past the wall of greenery.

The day after the mail carrier told her Elton had left, Essie started taking walks down the road as being good for her health. The walks took her past the opening in the hedge opposite the front door of the house next to hers.

So she saw the things go into the house. The drugstore delivered. The market delivered. "She must have a two-way door for that cat," Essie told Rake. "Cuz I see it around, but she never lets a thing out of the house. And where has she been this long time since he's gone?"

"For petesake. Now that he's left her for a younger woman you don't think she wants to talk about it do you? She stays inside until you come home."

Essie looked at the windows instead of the door next day and thought she saw Mrs. Belden standing back from the upstairs window. She hurried home, waited twenty minutes and walked out again. She was peering through the hedge opening when she saw in the yard the first movement she'd seen on her walks. A ladies' white glove was waving at her from the heap of Mrs. Belden on the ground. Essie hurried in and to the back corner of the house.

"Thank you for coming back," said Mrs. Belden.

"What are you trying to do?"

"I dropped my clippers. Can you help me up?"

"We better see if you're hurt." She had crumpled onto one side and looked in some way broken.

"Well, of course I'm hurt, lying here on the damp ground like this. But it's no hurt that lying here is going to help any."

"Is your house open?" Essie looked once at the tall house with the many windows.

"Course it's open or how would I get back in? Just pull me up. I'll be all right."

"Where's the phone?"

"You don't need to be calling the whole world because an old body fell down in her garden." She pushed her elbows into the ground to sit up but rolled back down again. "Well, you just let me rest another minute. My hip hurts."

Essie went to call a doctor. She was through the back stone entrance, past the clay pots, shovels and spades, and up the stairs to the main floor before she thought to be afraid she'd disappear. The house smelled of never being opened, of never letting out the smells of summers, winters, dinners, old wood fires. She felt the chill of its not being lived in and stood still a moment, not turning her head, pretending she wasn't looking around. Then she found the phone and the emergency numbers printed in large lettering. She waited for the doctor, hearing the old lady crawling across the green lawn making little "ah, ah" noises, hearing her open the screen door, which sighed and cracked, and fall through it onto the stone floor of the potting room, hearing her drag herself to the staircase, and the flap-thunk of each hand and knee as the old lady pulled herself, gasping, up the wooden stairs.

When the house was too quiet and Essie imagined the old lady about to fall through the door into the kitchen so she felt she could not hold onto the phone any longer, the doctor came on and said, "Doctor Parnell."

"Who?" Essie said. The old lady had not crashed into the kitchen. "Oh, yes, I mean. Mrs. Belden has had a fall and I'm afraid to move her."

"Did she fall down the stairs?"

"No. She's out in the garden. But her hip hurts and she can't sit up."

"I'll meet her at the hospital. I'll get an ambulance. Can you stay there until it comes?"

"Yes. I'll stay."

Mrs. Belden hadn't moved. Her glasses reflected the sky and the cedar tops. Two skies, two treetops, side by side in the pools of glass. Essie had found a pair of glasses once under the lilac bushes. The lenses weren't broken. She wondered what had happened to the person wearing them. He'd been old, no doubt. They were glasses an old person would wear. She thought he'd just dropped dead wearing them and whoever found him didn't find or even look for, the glasses. Maybe though, he hadn't died and the glasses had fallen out of his pocket when he was planting those lilac bushes to begin with. She thought maybe the rain had washed up the glasses.

"He gets me to the hospital, it'll be the end of me," Mrs. Belden said.

"I don't have to go over there now she's home," Essie told Rake. "But I found her after all." She wrapped the apple tart and started down the road. "After all," she said to herself, "I came out once already." But she hovered near the hedge opening before striding to the door.

From somewhere inside Mrs. Belden called, "Come in." Essie started away from the bell button she hadn't pushed yet, then reached back to push the button. When no one called "come in" again, she opened the heavy front door and let herself into the central hall of the house. "Good afternoon," Mrs. Belden called from a day couch by the front window in the right-hand room.

"Good afternoon."

Essie stepped to the doorway and bowed forward from the waist so her head, but not her feet was in the room.

"Nice of you to visit," Mrs. Belden said so that Essie was emboldened to step into the room and stand in front of a chair by the nearer front window. "Please sit down." Essie sat and then jumped up again to hold out the tart.

"How nice, thank you." Mrs. Belden motioned it onto a table that held a diary and a fountain pen and a soda cracker on a plate.

"Well, who's going to do for you now that you're home?"

"I'll manage."

"You fell and broke your hip," Essie said to remind her of the reality of the fact that she was lying on a daybed because she had just come from the hospital where they had put a pin in her hip as Essie had heard from the mail carrier. "Can't be walking around on it." Essie sat back from the edge of her chair and frowned at the very notion.

"The hip gave out. Then I fell. Because I was perfectly all right one minute—and I never fall—the hip just gave out."

"Either way. I know you shouldn't be walking on it. Isn't the visiting nurse coming?"

"Oh, I suppose so. Dr. Parnell contacted the world before letting me home. I thought the place would be the death of me. But you see I've made it back though the garden must look just awful."

"I'll look for the clippers."

"No, no. Let it be." Essie let it be, thinking the clippers had perhaps become one of those things that years from now somebody would find and wonder about as she did about those glasses.

"At least I can visit," Essie told Rake and took Mrs. Belden's suppers to her in a covered dish. "She can't get about yet and all I ever see for her to do is her diary. Though maybe it makes good reading if she writes everything she has time to."

"You know those clippers?" she said to Rake, coming home in the evening a month later, coming from behind the hedge and appearing on the road and then inside her own house. "Well, she had them to hand. Big as life with the diary and when I asked where they'd been found she said the nurse took them from the potting room for her. But she told me back then that she'd lost her clippers."

"Well, she didn't lose them when she fell if they were in the potting room."

"Then why did she say she did? And she had on white gloves that day which has always bothered me because you don't clip wearing white gloves. You wear white gloves to church."

And again Mrs. Belden was on the lawn in white gloves but farther back in the garden part with a folding chair that she had apparently held onto to get that far and toppled out of because it was lying on its side in the same direction as Mrs. Belden was lying on hers. This time the clippers were on the grass, too.

"Well you just rest there a minute now," Essie told the still form though she could tell Mrs. Belden had died. "I'll go make that call." She called from Mrs. Belden's front hall where she'd called from the last time.

The diary was on the table snapped shut. "Just to see if she says about those gloves or about those clippers." It was not as if the diary belonged to anyone anymore now that Mrs. Belden had died. Essie felt that she almost had permission to open it, even, that the dying had set it free.

Essie flipped the pages forward and back, but the dates for this year were not filled in past the spring. She read toward the beginning, "Elton is ailing and will not see the doctor. Bessie had her kittens but hasn't brought them out yet." Several days of chores and gardening, "deutzia blossoming." Then, "Refuses any treatment. Much pain." That was last spring before Elton left her for the other woman. "Found Bessie's kittens. Drowned all. Elton brought home pistol. In desk drawer. I hate a gun." Several more days. "I should have been quicker because he was waiting but at the last it took a long time to squeeze the trigger."

It took a long time to get back out of the house and to be back on the lawn and even so, Essie was partly in the sun-lit parlor by the chair by the window, would now, because of what she knew, be always partly inside that house.

"They'll be coming," she said to Mrs. Belden and looked to pick up the clippers where it was getting dark under the hedge and the cedar trees. The white gloves looked bright in the fading light.

The stems and stalks and leaves had quite taken over the garden. She did not see the clippers and had to poke the weeds around with her toe. "This time I saw those clippers," and poked with her hands farther into the tangle. What she grasped when she touched it was Elton's walking stick with the metal knob.

Dropping it and backing off, "There he is. There he is," she thought. "He doesn't need his cane. And she doesn't need those clippers either." She bumped the chair and caught her breath and turned and fled from the house, the garden, the white gloves.

In the dark she dug soil from the vegetable garden and spread it around the base of the lilacs and tamped it down. "Lest the rain wash too much away from there," she told Rake.

GRANDPA

I t was the time of night to walk out to the lane to look for bunnies and for deer. Carley walked out to see her grandfather. Her parents had gone over to the singing club picnic and the house seemed empty and full of white light.

When she came into the driveway she saw the tractor and trailer under the butternut tree with several lengths of wood on next to the stack of cord wood. She called, "Grandpa, Grandpa," the way she always called coming in. When she was little she called, "Grandpa, Grandma," but her grandmother had died two years ago when Carley was twelve. Now she called, "Grandpa," and he would come out from working.

It looked to her as if the door was off the house and leaning against the clapboards. She came closer, past the barn and the garden, and the door was off the house and leaning against the clapboards.

She called again, more loudly in case he was out in the field or whistling to himself. She stepped up the stone step and stuck her head inside the doorway and saw he was sitting in the rocking chair that had the green cushion. At first she thought he was dead and thought that couldn't happen. Then she saw he must be asleep. She stepped inside and came up to him softly so she wouldn't startle him.

Then she backed away and said, "Grandpa?" He didn't stir. He didn't move his arms in his lap and pick up his head and shake it. "Grandpa," she said sternly, but her mind was already flying out the door, touching the place in the woods where they went to cut firewood, the place at the edge of the field where there were blueberry bushes, the place in the field where the deer stood still when they came up the lane, looking for where he could be if he wasn't here.

It touched on the tractor and the trailer hitched together by the woodpile under the butternut tree. "I can't leave you here," she said in the soft voice she used for talking when there were deer and bunnies in the lane. "In the dark with the door off the house," and she thought she would have to take him home.

She looked again at her grandfather sitting alone in front of her and thought how she had known when she'd come in that he was dead. "Why did you take the door off, Grandpa?"

Carley went out the open door. Summer squash in the garden were ready to be picked, three of them, small the way she liked them. She picked the three, put them on the edge of the grass and weeded along the row of beets. Not much to weed, a few of pussley and lamb's-quarters, none of them big. Then she thinned down the row of beets and had a handful of young ones and greens. She kept going to the barn and past it to where he had the tractor standing out next to the cord wood pile with the trailer hitched on. So she didn't have that to do, back the tractor in to the tree trunk where the tongue of the wagon rested, back in and line up with the drawing bar on the tractor.

She hoped the electric start would work because she had never cranked it by herself. It did work and the tractor noise started up in the night. She drove across the lawn to the house, the trailer following. It took two tries to line up with the open door, then she backed the trailer up to the door and wedged on the brake and left the tractor running. Its sound hit up against the clapboards and came back down on her.

Carley climbed down onto the drawing bar and up the trailer onto the several long pieces of firewood he hadn't unloaded onto the cord wood pile and worked across those to the doorsill.

Then she crossed the flat floor to him. "Come on, Grandpa. I'll take you," she said to him. She took the afghan from the couch. He seemed very small to her. She thought she was going to be afraid to touch him, but she wasn't afraid yet. She put the afghan around him.

Carley hadn't thought about it when he was standing, moving around, but she thought now, there wouldn't be much weight to him. He was about the same size she was. She took hold of the front rung on each side of his legs and, moving backwards, pulled the rocking chair across the floor toward the door. There was a little gap between the doorsill and the trailer, but she was afraid if she backed the trailer closer, she'd bump the sill. She edged the chair forward so the rockers were on the sill and she could tip the chair onto the wood. "Oh, Grandpa," she said. "I can't."

It would have been easier to, as she'd planned, lift up the back rockers until he toppled out of the chair forward, but she wouldn't do it. She went around behind the rocker and into Grandpa's bedroom, got his two pillows and the blanket folded at the bottom, and climbed past the rocker through the doorway and onto the wood.

The tractor threw its spurts of sound against the house and in through the doorway. Grandpa didn't move in the chair. She made a place in the wood for him to lie down on the blanket and pillows. Then she put a foot on the trailer and a foot on the doorsill.

She reached for him wrapped in his afghan and touched him. He was an old man, she saw, her grandfather. She thought if she could rock him forward it would help her lift him so she went through the doorway and around the rocker and backed it off the sill and went through the doorway and straddled the space between it and the trailer. Then with the foot on the sill she pushed down on the rocker and the chair tipped forward. Her grandfather fell against her, and wasn't light, but already falling toward the pile of wood or the space between her feet, and she lifted and stepped her weight onto the trailer and he came with her and stumbled down onto the bed she'd made, and she landed next to him on the wood and pulled her arm from under him. She'd banged her leg on the places where he'd lopped branches off the wood. His blanket didn't cover the back of him so she tucked the other blanket up around him, and his head was on the pillows.

Carley got up and stepped through the doorway and pulled the rocking chair back to its place. She wanted to sit in it a moment before they left. Her legs had lost their strength.

But she climbed back along the load and onto the drawing bar, up onto the seat and put the tractor in gear, set off the brake. At the garden, she stopped and climbed down over the wheel and picked up the squash and beet greens and climbed up the drawing bar, put the vegetables in a hollow by the front of the load and climbed into the tractor seat.

It was past the time they would have seen bunnies or deer. She pulled on the headlights and started down the driveway. The air was crisp coming past her. She drove the tractor on the road the way they drove the tractor on the road to get gas at the gas station, in third gear with the throttle pushed forward. Her hair tugged around the back of her head.

She had the feeling Grandpa was standing on the drawing bar holding onto the rim of the tractor seat and they were going in for gas. When they went in for gas it was daytime and they'd feel the maple trees pass overhead and open into sunlight. She would hold onto the tractor seat and look down between her feet on the drawing bar and watch flecks in the road skin past.

He could be on the drawing bar behind her. The hair tugged at the back of her head in the breeze she made.

They went under the maples and came out to the open. The sky was pale and turning darker, and the stars stayed way up high. She came onto the main road and went down past Baker's and Ziebron and Blakeslee, set back from the road and with lights in the windows.

She kept going. A soft whistling came from behind her. He was sitting on the load, then, facing forward and watching her back, watching for her to turn and look, watching to see her face. Her shoulders were rigid; her back, a pressed board. She pushed the gas up a notch and held, stiff-armed to the steering wheel.

He wasn't on the drawing bar. He was in the trailer whistling "When You Wore a Tulip."

The hair tugged at the back of her head, but she didn't turn around.

When she thought she must turn around, with the tractor still going forward drawing on to the gas station, she pursed her lips and burst the air through them, but she didn't whistle. She tried to whistle but the air got blown away from her lips. Her mouth was dry. And then she wet it up and whistled along with him, "In the Good Old Summertime."

Coming in under the stars and beneath the maples with half a load of firewood and her grandfather on the back, she came down the main road, driving at near top speed. The tunes she was whistling flew back over the road and the tractor kept coming on. She drove stiff-armed and she whistled high where her Grandpa couldn't reach, and he went down for the low notes where she couldn't touch them.

She drove into the gas station and stopped with the tractor running. The twin was buried down in under the hood of his car pulled up alongside the plate glass window where the light shone out so he still had the office open.

Carley sat on the tractor seat looking straight ahead where the road closed down to make a lane through the trees. She tried to whistle through the sobs that smoothed down from her shoulders through her body and shook her against the hard rim of the tractor seat. She held on to the steering wheel and looked over it at the exhaust pipe sticking straight up from the tractor. Then she pulled out and drove home to her house. She stopped the tractor and trailer in front on the street because as far as she knew Grandpa had never driven into any driveway other than his own.

T here's poison ivy all over that place. You can't get anywhere near."

"What I thought, see, is I'd wear this beekeeping outfit." They were leaning up against the off side of Kent's truck in the sanded out area of the parking lot at the corner coffee. Kent moved off the door so Julius could look in and see the khaki suit with the helmet and veil on top of it.

"Where'd you get that?"

"Oh, you know? George Wadhams used to have bees and he swapped all his equipment to Jesse Gates in trade for his hammerin' anvil. Well, Jesse already had one suit of his own so I traded him that small vise I had in the barn for this set."

"Know who has a nice anvil is Durr Stone," Julius said.

"Yeah. Got it from George Wadhams. Only reason George wanted the anvil was he wanted Durr's drill press."

"Only reason you wanted that suit . . ."

"Was to get near enough to poison ivy to bring some nice copper tubing back into circulation. Shame to see it going to waste and ruining the economy."

"How much you think he's got?" Julius said.

"When he was still collecting had at least a ton. Hard to tell. I helped him unload what he salvaged from the Tripp job and that was years ago."

"What'd he do, plant the poison ivy around it?"

"Hell, no. Just dropped it in where it was already growing. Spot in his back field, a little lower than the rest, somewhat in the shade. Good conditions."

"Well, I heard of the copper. And I heard of the poison ivy, too. How come he never traded it in?"

"Well, that's a good question," Kent said. "You see, the whole time he was dropping it into there he never got poison ivy. Said he could roll in it, but he didn't. Then we were cutting off that woodlot down by the river, and one of the trees was full of poison ivy. We were all wearing gloves and all, but he says he'll take down the firewood and cut it up. Working without his shirt, he was, and the chain saw flinging spits of ivy juice. Shoulda seen him. Welts all over his chest and arms. Had goggles on or it woulda got his eyes.

"After that he traded any copper he got to Sid at the Scrap Yard right off the truck. Got the going price. This old stuff, though. Worth a dollar to every dime it was worth then."

"Funny how some people never get it when they're kids and get it later."

"Yeah. Some of us kids growing up, though. We got it all the time."

They tipped up their coffees and threw the empties into the back of Kent's truck. "We'll take the Chevy," he said. "Meet me on the road at nine. It'll be dark enough by then."

"What made you decide to go after it now?"

"Read in the paper Pops Grimbach died in Florida couple days ago. He doesn't own it anymore. And nobody else owns it yet. Might's well be us."

"Nice of him to wait for summer," Julius said.

Kent picked Julius up on the road at 9:25 in a World War II four-wheel drive Army Chevy truck with its lights on.

"You got gas in it this time?" Julius said and climbed off the running board into the cab.

"Always got gas in it. Just never know how much."

"Get you any tires yet?"

"You don't appreciate the difficulties finding good used parts for a classic like this."

"Tires looked pretty slick time we got stuck outta gas out by Ely's pond."

"Haven't worn through yet."

Kent turned off the main road and headed out north toward Winchester. When he came to the lane of maples he turned off on to Old Cart and drove four miles between the field rock stacked on each side to make a stone wall. Then he turned into a field.

"Get out and move that gate," he said, and Julius dropped down out of the truck and swung the pole down from where it was resting from one stone to the other across the opening. Kent drove through and Julius replaced the pole. He climbed back in and they crossed the first field.

The field looked white as the lights hit it. Hadn't grown up yet to the first cutting. Where the lights hit the trees at the back of the field, they could see trunks and lower green leaves with black shadows. Above that the trees were all black. Kent headed for the lane through the woods to the back field, going slightly downhill now. The lights found the opening and he turned the truck into the lane.

Along the lane, standing on both sides, were washing machines, refrigerators, iceboxes, several white stoves, and one cast-iron rust one with the stove pipe still standing in it, box springs and mattresses standing, leaning, filling in, cars and car parts at the end.

"Whew," Julius said. "Where'd he get all those?"

"More than in his lifetime."

"Lined up just like an audience for when we went through," Julius said.

"Yeah. We're the biggest attraction in years."

They came out into the back field and Kent swerved around the one more truck that was at the top of the slope.

"Couldn't fit it into the lane," he said.

"That the one he swapped Ely for to use it for parts?"

"Looks like."

"Stop a minute. Let's take a look." Kent stopped the truck and Julius dropped down out and walked back to look. "He's taken every good thing off of it. Only thing on it is the body and the wheels. Still got the tires on, but I don't guess they're any good if he didn't swap them onto something else."

The field was lighter than the lane and Kent drove around the edge going slow, looking for the poison ivy.

"Used to have a truck like that," Julius said. "Good running truck. Yep. Over 200 thousand on it. Took it apart to change the rings. Number four piston came right apart in my hand. Seven pieces. Was still running though before I took it apart. Couldn't get the pieces all back in right. Had to replace the piston. Sold it to Sam'el Aldrich. Got the one I got now from Jensen."

"Don't ever buy a vehicle from Jensen." Kent flicked on the low beams and scouted the low end of the field.

"Boy, don't I know it. Trying to swap it now for the tractor Buck's got on his lawn with the For Sale."

"Yeah. Well, don't ever tell him that Jensen had it, even looked at it." He stopped the truck. "Was right along in here. Get out and look. I'll back up so's you can use the beams."

The pile was under the edge of the tree boughs. The tubing wasn't stacked in any order, just thrown crisscross off the truck and left the way it landed. The ivy grew up through it with the small starts of maple trees. Behind the pile, brush had grown up, maple saplings and dogwood, beech, filling in under the grown trees. The ivy looked bright green and lush in the headlights.

"Couldn't a found a meaner place to stash the stuff, could he? How was he fixing to ever get it out?"

"Had a skidder for working the woodlot. Figured he could skid it out in a bunch just like the logs."

"Well it won't be easy loading. Where's the skidder?"

"Traded it to Jesse Gates for that one-lunger and saw arbor he used for cord wood and the Mustang he'd just restored for his wife."

"Oh, yeah. I remember that."

Julius stayed on the ground and backed Kent in in the truck.

"Looks good right there," he hollered.

Kent cut the motor and opened the door. "Christ," he said and swung back in and jumped on the starter. The truck roared on again. "Forgot I want to leave her running. Doesn't always start right up." He killed the lights and swung down again.

"Lights helped back here a little bit, I think," Julius called over the noise of the engine. Kent pulled them on again.

"Watch out," Kent hollered and dived back into the driver's seat. Julius ran to the passenger's door. In the headlights they watched the parts truck come bouncing down the field toward them. They didn't move. It had cut loose and started slow but it was already fast bouncing toward them. Kent was in the driver's seat and Julius was on the other running board and they held on. The truck was headed toward Kent's side and coming fast. Then it was there. There was a high CHING and the driver's door slammed shut and the truck hit the pile of copper and ivy and rolled right up onto it and fell in and came to a stop against the wall of brush, bending the saplings back at the bottom.

After it stopped, they waited for the motion of everything else to stop.

"Boy, I thought we had it that time," Julius said. "I thought we had it good."

Kent climbed out the passenger door. "Over a couple of feet and it would have blown up the works," he said.

"What d'you suppose tore that thing loose?" Julius said. "Suppose we rattled it loose?"

"Who knows? Probably been standing there for years, aimed at the copper. Waiting for a coupla clowns like us to run over."

Kent got into the legs of the beekeeping uniform and pulled it up across his shoulders to stick his arms in.

"Mosquitoes are getting me something fierce," Julius said. Kent pulled the net down over his face.

"Well," Julius said. "How we gonna get four tons of copper out from under two tons of scrap metal?"

"Either gonna have to push it farther or haul it back off."

"Can't push it farther."

"Unless we cut down the brush."

"Would be fairly noticeable."

"Right. So let's haul it back."

"You got a rope?"

"Yep. Rope in the back."

Kent looped the rope around the back bumper of the parts truck and hitched the two loop ends to the hitch on the Chevy bumper. He climbed into the driver's seat and took off the gloves before he touched the steering wheel. In low gear he started the Chevy inching forward.

"Okay," Julius called when he had the rope taut between the bumpers, and Kent gave it some gas and dug in. The parts truck gave a lurch and he gave the Chevy more gas and creamed up the field with the bumper bouncing crazy on the end of the rope.

Kent stopped the truck, and Julius got the rope and the bumper off, and Kent backed back down.

"Try the axle," he hollered out the window over the noise of the truck. The taillights lit the ivy up red.

"Not me," Julius hollered back. "You're the one wearing the outfit."

"Jesus Christ." Kent tramped on the brake and left it in neutral. He had to leave the helmet off to get in under the parts truck, but he put on the gloves.

"Ground still seems soft there," Julius said when he crawled out and hooked up to the bumper.

Kent looked where he had slicked down the grass pulling out. "Okay," he said.

Julius eased him forward till the rope was taut, and Kent gave it some gas pedal and rocked the parts truck off of the copper and partway up the field. He couldn't leave it though or it would roll. He towed it to the other low corner and let it nose into the brush there. Julius came running up and let loose the towrope. He stood up on the running board and they drove back across to the copper tubing and backed down in.

"Try and miss where you were before," Julius said. "You got it all dug up."

Kent settled the truck right back on it. "How can I see where I'm going without you telling me?" he said. "It'll be all right."

Then they started loading. Kent pulled some of the poison ivy off the top of the pile and pulled the copper tubing around out of there. And Julius, wearing his gloves, lifted what Kent tore loose onto the back of the truck. "We have to have the truck running while we do this?" Julius said. "Sure would be nicer without the exhaust."

"Better not chance it," Kent said. "Long as we've got her running."

The taillights made big dark holes in the shadows where Kent had pulled out pieces of the pile. The rest they colored dark red. The white ends of the ivy where Kent had torn the leaves off stood up out of the pile and whipped against his legs when he moved the tubing. A breeze came up and riffled through the tree boughs above them and moved the mosquitoes off. It helped carry the truck exhaust away from directly where they were working. They had the top of the pile ripped off and loaded onto the truck.

"How much more is there?" Julius said when they stopped to lean against the side of the truck and drink coffee from the thermos.

"Hard to tell. The truck'll carry whatever we want to put on though, so we'll just keep loading until we quit."

It wasn't that it was coming on to morning. It wasn't that because it was still the middle of the night. It was something subtler than that. It was like a change from first night to later night. A mist came down like the start of rain but it didn't rain. It wet down the grass and then stopped, and the breeze dropped, and Kent helped lift the last of what he'd pulled free onto the truck and got in his side. Julius got in the passenger side.

"All right." They pulled from the thermos. Kent put the truck in low gear, gave it some gas, and the back end dug into the slick grass under the tires.

"Your drive's all right. It's the tires that'll get you," Julius said. "Why don't you let off the brake?"

Kent let off the brake, and the truck walked up a little and slid to the side. The slide was so small they almost didn't notice. But it did it again, the tires slipping on the wet grass and on the slick small smooth place Kent had made with the tires.

"Jesus Christ," he said. "Come on, don't fail me now." He shifted into second and tried to glide out, but the truck moved farther to the side.

"You're gonna end up in the bushes, you go much farther," Julius said. "You do that and you'll never back out."

"Oh, Christ," Kent said.

A little more mist came down. It wasn't hard enough to call rain. They sat in the cab of the truck and watched it hit the windshield, drift into the headlights of the truck.

"You think you could pull out without the load?"

"Hell, yes."

"I don't know. Usually have better traction weighted down, don't you think?"

"Not the traction. It's the load. Sinking in too deep. Making mush out of the ground."

No rain was hitting into the headlights. It was steamy in the truck cab. They opened the windows.

"You don't have a longer rope?" Julius said.

"Got a chain."

"How long?"

"Twenty feet."

"Might do it," Julius said. Kent stared straight through the front windshield. "Hitch up to the parts truck, load it and pull from the top of the rise, you got yourself a skidder."

"Further than twenty feet up the hill," Kent said.

"Yeah. Look though. This is the boggy part. It's firm ground above and not as steep. It's only steep right here."

They unloaded the copper tubing onto the ground next to the pile, and the truck walked sideways across the hill away from it. They hitched the chain to the parts truck back axle and hauled it to the top of the slope. They hitched the chain to the front axle and from up the slope let it back down to the copper pile. The steering wanted to do something ornery, but Julius got in and stood where there was no seat and rigged the steering.

"Damn near no floorboards," he hollered. "I thought I'd fall through and run me over."

They left the Chevy in neutral with the parking brake on and loaded the parts truck down onto its shot springs.

"I didn't want to tell you this while we were still loading," Julius said. "But I thought you'd notice it was sorta quiet."

It was lighter in the field than behind the parts truck next to the poison ivy. The Chevy headlights pointed across the field and the taillights shone a red area around the back bumper and hit the grass.

"Oh, hell and damn," Kent said.

"Stopped a few minutes ago."

"Oh, hell."

"Did you bring along some gas?"

"Course I brought along some gas. You think I carry around empty five gallon gas containers with no gas in them?"

Julius looked up at the stars. "That time at Ely's pond was an exception," Kent said. Julius dug into the cab from the passenger side and came out with the five gallon can.

"Damn it," Kent said. "Only thing is. Run outta gas this thing won't start causa no gas in the carburetor. Run's itself dry."

He hauled the gas container up to where the filler spout stuck off the side about six inches, climbed onto the running board, and pulled off the gas cap. "Here's the cap," he handed it to Julius. The gas cap was about four inches across and Julius made no remark about the size of the filler spout it uncovered.

"Don't lose it," Kent said, "and when I get down you pour that gas in, put on the top, and get outta the way." He trickled some gas down the filler spout and handed the can to Julius. "Got to pressure some gas into the fuel pump." Julius stepped back with the can.

Kent had his whole face down over the huge filler spout, covering it with his mouth, sealing it off with his cheeks, blowing down hard, breathing in the air through his nose and blowing it down hard onto the gas in the line to force it up to the fuel pump.

Julius moved around to the side of him to see it better. "I don't believe it," he said and got to laughing.

Kent's face puffed up as he blew down into the filler spout. He pulled his face back and gas erupted in slashing peaks around the rim of the spout and he was wiping gas off his face, all red from blowing and sputtering. "You made me laugh," he hollered. "You made me laugh." He was wiping off his face with the red flag from the lumber yard and had to spit some out besides. "Christ, you made me laugh," he sputtered, dragging the oily rag over his face. He opened the hood and climbed onto the grill work then with the five gallon can and poured a tease down into the carburetor, leaning in over the engine works, balanced on the grill. Then he climbed down and hauled himself up into the driver's seat. "Take that and tip it into the spout now. I'll try to start her. Battery's got a dead cell."

He climbed into the driver's seat and jumped on the starter. The truck woofed twice, gently, not very loud. He jumped down and climbed the grill again. "Give me that can." He trickled the last of the gas into the carburetor.

"Not going to do it, is she?" Julius said.

"Oh, sure she will. Almost caught that first time. I could hear it." Julius took the gas can. Kent jumped on the starter and sound beat up into the night. "Get in here," Kent hollered. "Get that tank aboard and get in here."

Julius jumped onto the running board, swung the can in through the open window. Kent got the truck into gear and let off the brake and put down the gas and they started forward, the Chevy with Julius outside, and the chain and, last, the parts truck. Kent had it in low and headed for the break in the trees. The truck lights were on. The night smelled like gasoline and exhaust.

They came to the top of the hill. They came to the lane. "Can't take the truck. That isn't ours." They unloaded the copper tubing from the parts truck into the back of the Chevy and now the night was changing into morning.

"I don't know, coulda fit a lot more," Kent said.

"Never mind."

Birds started going crazy in the trees, calling back and forth, filling up the trees with noise, excitement. Light was coming up around them.

Kent got into the cab and Julius climbed onto the running board on the passenger side. He had hold of Kent's red flag from the lumber yard. They started into the lane. Kent drove slowly. Julius hung onto the window frame and leaned way out holding the red flag and waving it. Kent waved and smiled through the windshield, sitting back in the seat and driving with his arm looped over the steering wheel. The refrigerators, the stoves, were lined up on both sides of the lane. The mattresses leaned against each other. The birds clamored. Kent swaggered his head behind the steering wheel. The tree branches moved in the breeze.

At the end of the lane Kent stopped the truck and let Julius climb in.

"Let's go." Julius said. Kent shifted into second.

"Want to . . ."

"Never mind. I'm BUSY tonight," Julius said. "You just better hope Sid at the Scrap Metals was one of those not allergic to poison ivy or he'll know real fast where you got this load."

"Oh, Sid. He was one of those kids . . . ," Kent's voice got very quiet, "just had to look at it."

The truck slowed down without Kent's foot on the gas pedal and came to a stop. Kent put in the clutch so it wouldn't stall.

MERLE'S AND MARILYN'S MINK RANCH

From the porch of Merle's and Marilyn's Mink Ranch, Marilyn and Junior watched the black truck with the wide chrome grill and the man driving it, wearing a hat—in this heat getting ready to rain—made of what looked like mink with a tail down the back like a Davy Crockett hat and a vest with fringe cut to look like leather but looking, if you want to know, like soft and frayed old cardboard. That was Junior's brother and Marilyn's son. That was Bobby Joe.

Inside the truck, Bobby Joe stuck both elbows exactly across each other and latched his hands onto the steering wheel and wrenched it around so both his elbows were back straight in front of him and the truck tipped up the dust and gravel and slid around and without using his elbows this time, he stopped the truck and it banged back onto its springs and popped the door open and Bobby Joe landed on both feet next to it.

Junior sat in a chair on the porch with his feet up on what railing was left strumming some G, D, and Fs out of what looked like a cardboard guitar for "I Gave the Phone My Nickel but It Didn't Give Me You," a song he was making up about a pay phone. Junior didn't wear the whole ranch, but their mother, a wide woman with flat blonde hair dyed to the roots, who was sitting in one of the kitchen chairs at the kitchen table on the porch wearing a muumuu dress, and who wouldn't step into the truck with either of them, ever, never mind what they were wearing or where they were going—she just wouldn't do it—WAS Merle's and Marilyn's Mink Ranch because there wasn't any longer any Merle.

A spat of rain flattened some of the dust on the driveway into rocks that looked like gravel. Bobby Joe stopped stretching his arms above his head and shaking his head back and forth inside the hat with the tail and leapt across the step to the porch.

"What if the sheriff comes acrost you driving like that and pulling into this driveway?" Marilyn said and her words fell over the edge of the porch and landed flat with the rain and gravel leaving dust spots between them.

"Aw, Ma. That ever happens, then I'll put the sheriff sign in the window and see what they say." Bosco, down at the used car parts, had given him the white license tag that said sheriff in black letters when Bobby Joe had gone down there for the used tires to make the fountain Marilyn had on the grass.

"Don't go thinking that's your truck now, will you," Junior kept plucking at the guitar but stopped blowing wet ginger cookie through a harmonica long enough to tell him.

Marilyn said, "You stop that."

Bobby Joe finished the stretch he'd started out on the driveway, jumped back down across the step and slammed the truck door. He jumped back onto the porch through the gap in the railing that Junior had made riding his Norton motorcycle out of the house and off the porch when the cat dropped onto his back from the upstairs landing the first day the door was open in March when the snow had melted to slush and tire tracks.

Marilyn wouldn't look at either one of them. She was watching the fountain in the yard. After Merle died, she had made the fountain from truck tires and auto tires cut and painted white and stacked like a wedding cake to about eight feet tall. It was not something anyone missed driving by. She thought it drew attention to the sign for Merle's and Marilyn's One-of-a-kind Mink Ranch. It drew attention to itself, filled with Easter grass and pinwheels and Christmas tinsel to simulate water and with Christmas ornaments on the edges of each tier.

"No phone is going to take a nickel in this day and age," Bobby Joe said to Junior, and Junior slammed his feet down off the railing and the chair leg knocked over the beer bottle that foamed around the floorboards. Junior kicked it at the space between the railings, but it hit the bottom rail and rolled back at him and he kicked it again and it sailed clear through the open space, arcing the last of the foam across some dattered ferns, and Junior swung the guitar in the direction of Bobby Joe. Bobby Joe tore the letter basket off the wall next to the open front door and held it in front of him like a shield and caught the harmonica in it when Junior threw it at him with his teeth.

Then Bobby Joe threw the basket and Junior whacked it with the guitar and it skidded across the top of the kitchen table past Marilyn and off the other end where it landed behind the cat. The cat, which had leapt to the porch and hunkered when the beer bottle landed in the ferns, exploded back through the missing railing and scrambled up the sideboard of the truck where she sat and licked her paw.

Inside the house, upstairs, Bobby Joe sounded like tearing over bureaus. "That's one last time with the guitar," he shouted and Junior stood, panting, holding the guitar by the neck with his fingers and thumb, letting it hang toward the porch floor, and not stepping into the dust from the yard that had settled in the house where Bobby Joe called down, "I'm leaving outta here."

"Didn't he make me, Ma?" Junior said. "You saw that."

Then a sound from upstairs and something hit the porch roof and skittered down it and dropped from the roof onto air that didn't hold it and collapsed onto itself past where the railing was missing to the ferns—a cardboard wood-grain wardrobe open to the metal hangers that clashed and settled with it and released the rain which began to ping against it and turn it into what it already looked like—something chewed and sodden.

"All right," Junior said. "You see?"

A flock of twisted wire hangers flew down and turned the yard dark and rain buried the beer bottle and stood the gravel up in puddles.

Marilyn watched the fountain. Rain hitting the Christmas tinsel made it look like falling water.

Junior put the guitar onto the table, ignored the space between the railings and the wet and folded cardboard and the rain, and walked deliberately down the porch steps to trade in the truck that Bobby Joe had got for the motorcycle. He yanked open the truck door. He rolled up the window and stepped onto the running board and, using the steering wheel, swung onto the seat. He turned the key in the ignition and the large U that hung from the key chain swung back and forth.

He couldn't hear if the truck had started in the rain so he turned the key again and the truck chuttered and he let the key go and slid his foot off the clutch.

Upstairs in the space where he had taken the window out of the frame to get the wardrobe out, Bobby Joe stepped onto the windowsill and held the window frame on both sides and leaned out into the rain.

"You get outta that truck," he hollered, but the truck was bucking against the clutch. Junior had never driven anything except the Norton when he had had it, and all of his attention was on the steering wheel clutched in his fists.

The truck bucked in first gear and left a space in the driveway for the rain. Marilyn watched the fountain spout and trickle.

Bobby Joe leaped out the window onto old and wet roof shingles and slid down them to the edge and with his feet straight in front of him and his elbows crossed as if on the steering wheel, filled for a moment the space in the air between Marilyn and the fountain before he landed, feet first in the tangle of wire hangers and soggy cardboard.

Sitting in the collapsed wardrobe in his vest with the cardboard fringes, Bobby Joe slapped rain off his hat and shoulders.

Junior got the truck to the end of the driveway where he slammed it into reverse and leaped it backwards over the puddle collecting where the driveway met the road and onto the grass through ruts of its own making and stopped in the fountain which toppled, part of it onto the lawn and part of it against the sideboard and into the back of the truck.

Junior turned off the ignition and sat still looking straight ahead through the windshield. Bobby Joe sat straight still in the wardrobe and stopped slapping at the rain.

"Aiee," Marilyn called and stood up from the kitchen table in a heave that tipped the guitar off the top onto the porch.

"Aiee," she had her arms wide over her head and dashed down the porch steps to the driveway. Rain slapped into the roots of her hair and laid them flatter against her head. Rain made dark fringes down her dress and she flung herself onto the center of the fountain where motion of the rain flapped the Easter grass and tinsel.

Marilyn threw the dress off over her head and tried to cover what looked like a valise by working the valise up inside the dress.

Rain hit her wide undershorts and back and the wide strip of elastic and hooks that held down the straps from over her shoulders and, in stop motion, Junior looked through the windshield and Bobby Joe looked at the kitchen table on the porch where she had been.

Marilyn gathered up the dress and floundered out of the fountain and neither of her sons watched her climb the porch and step over the doorsill into the dust from the yard that had settled in the house.

Bobby Joe climbed slowly out of the wardrobe and in his wet clothes crossed the yard to the truck.

Junior rolled down the window and Bobby Joe opened the door and pulled him out. He climbed into the truck and started it and pulled it forward off the fountain and turned it off. The fur of his hat was stuck in points around his head.

"You know it isn't money," he said through the open window to Junior.

"Nope. Isn't money."

"If it were money," Bobby Joe said, "we'd go get your motorcycle."

"Yep. But it isn't."

"You think we better build the fountain?"

"You think we better let her put whatever that was back inside?"

"I don't think so."

Bobby Joe dropped out of the truck.

Marilyn came back out of the house with her dress back on and carrying a cardboard valise, the sides crimped into stitching around the edge and got into the truck on the passenger side and made them both get in and drive her to the cemetery where the other fountain she had constructed looked as near as she could make it to the fountain that she had at home.

"You come back here in two hours," she said. "Both of you. Don't either of you come alone."

Bobby Joe drove the truck to Merle's and Marilyn's Mink Ranch and pulled into the driveway and stopped by the wardrobe.

Without whatever it had had in the center holding it together, the fountain, when they put it back together, didn't look the same as it had. They hadn't put all the ornaments in the right places as some of them weren't the same as they had been before the truck tilted into them.

Rain thudded onto the cardboard that earlier it had struck

with sharp pip pips. Wet cardboard had rolled away from the thin wooden splints that had held the wardrobe together and the wooden splints, broken either by the fall from the roof or the fit through the window or before that, were bright wet in the dark fringes of bent and folded cardboard.

"Been two hours has it?"

"Been two hours."

"Raining pretty hard." Bobby Joe reached his hand for the beer bottle, and Junior said again, "It's empty."

"You think there's any in the one out there?"

"Don't think there's any."

"Might be though." Bobby Joe pulled himself forward by the edge of the kitchen table and still hunkered in the position he'd been seated, thrust himself through the gap in the railing, through the roll of rain falling from the porch roof, and found the beer bottle wet with rain on its green side in the ferns. He stood with it and tilted it and licked his tongue around the lip of it and holding it by his finger and thumb dropped it again to the ferns.

He put his hands on his hips to look at the wardrobe. Rain thudded into him. "You think we maybe oughta move this outta here?"

"Leave it," Junior said.

"Because when she comes back she's going to be awful mad that we didn't go and get her like she said. You think we maybe better oughta drag it around the other side?"

Junior said, "Take it back up the roof, why dontcha?" but he moved himself to the edge of the rain and looked out. "We could drag it," he said. "I'll take the hangers."

Bobby Joe dragged the cardboard wardrobe by one of the wooden splints that broke when he pulled it but he kept dragging until the cardboard fell apart from there. Then he took hold another place that came off in his hand. "I don't know," he said. "Maybe have to push it." He took hold two places and most of the wardrobe moved across the wet gravel and puddles of wet dust in the driveway and came with him around the corner of the house where the broken sofa stood on its arm next to a refrigerator, what they thought was a watering tank, and the gas cylinders for the stoves.

Junior brought the wire hangers and threw them high to come down like sparklers in the rain around the appliances. "Could go out for beer," he said.

"Could."

They walked along the scraped lines the wardrobe had made. Bobby Joe stamped down the pieces of cardboard that hadn't come with him around the house corner, and they climbed into the truck.

"You want to pick her up then?" Bobby Joe turned the key in the ignition.

"Might's well," Junior said. "Long's we're out."

"Whatever that was that she did have in the fountain you know won't be safe out there, whatever it was, wherever she put it."

"That's right," Junior said. "What we're going to have to do . . ."

"Is dig it up again from where she put it and put it back in here under the tires where it's safe." Bobby Joe pulled across the ruts the truck had made to the fountain. "May as well pick her up first then so she doesn't have to know about it."

The valise was there in the slick earth, this time, after they put Marilyn back at the kitchen table on the porch, her hands empty from wiping them on her dress in the rain halfway home.

"Not halfway," Junior said.

"Pretty close," Bobby Joe said and tipped over with the truck the fountain at the cemetery she had had to dig around under. "Because she wouldn't leave it above ground. Not here, away from home where she couldn't watch it."

The valise was there and the rain hit clean dimes onto the slick of earth on it on the truck tailgate.

"How we gonna set that back up?" Junior said. They had tipped the fountain over in one piece and it lay on wet grass. "You got some rope that we could pull it?"

"I don't think so."

"What kind of truck is it that doesn't have a rope?"

"I don't know yet what it has." Bobby Joe opened the passenger door and looked into the glove compartment. He slammed the door and went to the driver's side, opened the door and tipped the back of the seat forward. He slammed the door. "Doesn't have a rope," he said. "We could lift it. Two of us. Easy."

"Huh." Junior stamped some more on the ground that had been dug and undug and dug and covered and then they lifted the top of the rubber tire fountain to stand it.

"See?" Bobby Joe said. "Wouldn't have been safe there at all. Too easy."

"At least she put it underground, though." Junior rubbed his feet back and forth in the wet grass, left streaks of wet earth.

"Well." Bobby Joe stood next to the tailgate. "You think we oughta open it?"

Junior kept rubbing his feet on the grass. Rain left grimy spaces between the dimes it was hitting onto the valise.

Bobby Joe said, "See how much is there?"

"You think we ought to?"

Their hands wiped rain off the valise. "Inside."

Their four hands were on the valise, but Bobby Joe's hand was on the handle and the valise slid off the tailgate to his thigh. Junior walked with him to the driver's side.

"Oh, go get in," Bobby Joe said and got in and Junior crossed in front of the truck and got in. Rain slid onto the truck seat. Rain splattered the truck roof and windshield and hood.

"Is it locked?" Junior said.

"No locks." Bobby Joe opened both tabs at the same time with his thumbs and lifted the lid. Rain slid down to the seat. Junior looked over the lid and rain from his hair slipped down to the bills.

"What is it?" he said. "Red bills? Yellow? It's play money." Rain from his hair dripped into the valise.

"Well, maybe. I dunno."

"What is it? Something so big I don't recognize them? Come on. Those aren't tens and twenties. They're not the right size."

"Not for U.S., no. But look here. The writing is foreign." Bobby Joe didn't reach into the valise. He didn't point. Junior looked over the lid.

"Hmm. Could be foreign money. Maybe a fortune."

"Yeah. And maybe all told, fifty bucks. How do you know?"

"You think . . ." Junior said.

"Nobody around here going to take red or yellow dollars to give you that Norton. Nope. I do not think. That may be millions or it may be nothing. Government that issued 'em might be dead by now."

Rain slid from the roof down the windshield.

"You want to put it back?"

Bobby Joe looked out the back window at the fountain standing next to the Easter grass clinging to the back end of the sideboard on the truck. "Better take it home," he said. "How do we know?"

"You think she knows?"

"Not unless he told her," Bobby Joe said.

"You think he told her?"

"Did he tell her there were never any minks?" Bobby Joe turned the key in the ignition.

Junior set the cover down over the bills. Bobby Joe set the sheriff license plate in the windshield.

"You gonna tell her we moved it?"

Bobby Joe looked over at Junior. "Never told me this hat wasn't mink either. Nope. Gonna do it after dark."

From the porch of Merle's and Marilyn's Mink
Ranch, Marilyn and Merle watched a cardboard
box that Merle had left at the corner of the mink barn lift
itself off the ground and run around the rain barrel
toward them, stub a corner and somersault like tumble-
weed along the driveway. The box slammed itself against
the porch railing that at that time, when Marilyn first
lived there, went all the way around the porch except for
the space where it turned and went down the steps where
Merle Jr. was glued to the corner post standing up. Merle
Jr. let go and sat down.

Merle stood up off the railing and stretched his arms
over his head. His white T-shirt with the X of suspenders
on the back looked very white in the grey closing light.
"Severe thunderstorm warnings," he said. He crossed the
porch and sat in a chair next to where Marilyn sat on
cushions on the porch swing he had made by hanging the
flat metal spring of some old twin bed by chains from the
porch roof joists. He laid one hand across his lap and held
onto the pipe in his teeth with the other and tipped the
chair back against the house. "Tornado watch in effect."

"You think you should tack down the loose window in
the barn?"

Merle Jr. pulled himself up the corner post of the railing
and clung there.

"Can't think where I laid my hammer," Merle said.

"It's under the upholstered chair," she said. Merle had
fixed the back leg of the upholstered chair—which looked
to him like an old tin bathtub studded around the edges
with tacks to hold on the green fabric—by propping the
head of the hammer on the floor and the end of the handle
under the seat after he and Marilyn had broken the back
leg leaning heavy in the chair before Merle Jr. was born.

"Well, that's all right, then," he said. "We never sit in it."

On the porch in the dark, Merle Jr. crawled to Marilyn

and got into her lap and fell asleep, and they watched lightning flick on and off past the barn.

"Makes 'em nervous," Merle said, meaning the minks. "Lightning."

"Doesn't bother him a bit," Marilyn said, meaning Merle Jr.

"I told you that they're flighty critters. Fur will fall off if they're startled. He's going to start walking, that's two of you you're going to have to keep away from down there. Good thing they know me, all of them, since they were first born."

While Merle worked himself up not to tell her that the Foley Brass Mill had laid him off last week and that he'd been playing poker with some foreigner, betting the mink ranch against some foreign dollars and winning, Marilyn started to worry about the tornado coming through to flatten the mink barn down in back where she had never seen any minks except one who liked to sleep in the window, sometimes, that she could see from the back door while she hung out the clothes.

"Should we go down to the cellar, you think?" Marilyn said and thunder that crashed over the next lightning flash rolled up over the mink barn and past the porch and let loose big hard drops of rain onto the porch roof.

"We should go to bed, I should think probably, just as well as sit here in the dark with the lights off in case the power should go out. Cellar's going to have water in it, I shouldn't doubt."

Lightning walked around in the yard and rain streaked through it and Marilyn couldn't hear herself get out of bed for the thunder tumbling around the porch and, in her nightgown, she looked out the window to the barn where she could see in the next walk of lightning that the window that was loose had fallen partway open at the top of the lower sash.

She had never asked Merle whether minks could climb,

but she assumed they could since that one she saw sometimes lay asleep in the window on the ledge, and she could not imagine that minks would climb onto window ledges and slanted glass to get outside in weather like this but they were such flighty creatures.

When Merle went down to the barn to check what he called "our security," he came back smelling like mink barn, which to Marilyn smelled awfully much like turpentine or paint. She thought of the minks as dirty animals since the spots Merle got onto his barn clothes down there were sometimes dark and sometimes lighter, but didn't come out in the wash. When she hung those clothes on the line, she pushed them way out to the clothesline pulley on the post so they wouldn't be so noticeable.

Marilyn went down the stairs and outside to the porch and looked again.

The box that had flown against the railing was beaten into something sodden against the porch steps and cold air from the rain coming down lifted her nightgown chill against her legs. From thinking she would wake up Merle and tell him about the window, she began thinking he wouldn't take the hammer from against the chair leg and, since she wouldn't probably disturb them any more in the dark outside the window than they were already disturbed by the dark and light and loud and flying night, she went inside and leaned the chair against the wall and unwedged the hammer and took it with her to the porch.

The cardboard box said Fine Paints Warner on the only elbow still sticking up in the next lightning flash, and Marilyn stepped down the step and around it, and rain flattened her hair to her head and her nightgown to the rest of her and ran down her hand to the hammer and took her breath away.

Cats, she remembered they used to say, took a baby's breath away and could kill it, though she had never figured out how. Since Merle Jr. had been born, she had made the cat stay outside, and it twined around her legs whenever she stepped out to feed it and tried to trip her and make her drop the baby so it could sit on its chest and take its breath.

Lightning walked through the yard and pulled a wagon of thunder behind it. The paint can—that was probably the paint can Marilyn had seen Merle holding out the truck window away from the truck while he drove with his right hand on the wheel—skittered on its round sides around the rain barrel at the corner of the mink barn, stopped in the flash of lightning and skittered back, and in the next flash, spun around and stayed still.

She pushed her legs forward against the heavy cling of nightgown that pulled her breasts and came with the hammer to the window with the lower sash leaning toward the yard.

She waited for the lightning but when it didn't come, she reached to where she thought the window was and pushed it upward against the frame, and something hit it from the other side, and lightning stepped behind her, sent the chill up under her night gown, and she saw it was the cat, for Christ's sake, on the window ledge. At least it didn't look like a mink which she had only seen in pictures. She set the hammer on the ground against the barn foundation and, holding the window against the frame, slid it up, and the cat shot out through the space and landed somewhere past her and came back, as she slid the window down to contain the minks, and tried to trip her with its wet and prickled fur.

With one hand on the window, Marilyn leaned down for the hammer, and the cat in the dark put its paws against her arm and, in the instant that Marilyn was sure she didn't know what had a hold of her, before she realized that it was, of course, for Christ's sake, the cat, she leaped backwards from the hammer. The window, that had stayed in the frame until she had pushed it and let the shim fall out, leaped from the barn into the storm straight at Marilyn, who sensed it coming and leaped away and fell over the cat who jumped to the windowsill, as she saw in the next lightning when she saw also the sash on the ground in broken glass.

Thunder rolled the lightning away and the night was dark, full of very loud water falling in pieces from a lowered sky to press her into the yard where she was sitting in her nightgown.

She watched a dark space where the flighty creatures, if they could climb, would now climb out the window in the next lightning flash, but they didn't.

The cat had gone from the window ledge, inside or out, she couldn't tell, though inside she would have guessed if it had any sense. She left the window sash, which would be hard to explain, she saw, if she put it back in the window frame now, broken, with its glass in pieces on the ground.

Marilyn stood and her nightgown pulled her down. She pulled it away from sticking to her skin and the rain glued it back. She reached for the hammer and tipped against the barn where the window was out and put her hand against the window sill, and lightning in the yard showed up the tall oblong shapes of the place where the minks stayed.

Tall, she thought they were, maybe partitions, to keep them apart and something tippy about them. Marilyn held onto the windowsill, and lightning showed her the wooden legs on the oblongs, and she raised herself to the window ledge—where there was no broken glass because it was in the yard—and eased herself over.

The fur of whatever came against her legs was wet and pointy so she knew it was, for Christ's sake, the cat again and brushed her legs through it, feeling her way with her feet and hands in the barn that smelled of turpentine and lightning. And the next lightning with rain pounding the roof showed her the easels with different sized canvases and boards.

She didn't walk around then, didn't look at all for the minks she knew she wouldn't find.

Lightning pulled the wagons farther off, and Marilyn crossed the yard, kicked into the cardboard box, moved around it and climbed to the porch and pulled her nightgown off over her head and the hammer in her hand and put the hammer back under the upholstered chair.

A clear day after rain made everything clean to Merle as if he weren't pretending anything. Water ran down the yard toward the barn in sunshine and made gullies with bright stones on the bottom. When he opened the wooden hatch, there was water in the cellar. Sunlight slid down and floated on it and went through and made the dirt floor look clear like a stream bottom. Clear like a stream he remembered near his grandfather's cabin in the woods and made him of a sudden feel that he could tell her. But, if he told her, no, if he told her then she would have to pretend to Merle Jr. It would be unfair then, and what if some night when he was older and asking questions, and Marilyn was having a beer on the porch, she forgot herself and said something. No. She would just feel purely terrible and so he set the hatch back down over the water.

Merle called Marilyn to the cellar hatch.

Marilyn thought he must know that she had discovered his secret, that something as big as that he had to know about her and that it could be easy to say, "Okay. Relax. It's all right," the way her grandmother did for her when she was living with her and going out the window onto the porch roof to see Merle. "Okay. Just go out the front door, will you, so I don't think you'll break your neck."

But the barn hadn't blown down and so she didn't say it and Merle lifted the cellar door again and said, "Just wanted to show you some of the sparkle," and closed it and didn't tell her.

Everything looks so still at night in the middle of the night, Marilyn was thinking in the downstairs bedroom she had taken after Merle died, looking at the soft dust crumples at the legs of the bureau, at the grey light that ran away from the shaded lamp into a cobweb stretched in the corner where she could reach it with a broom every time, she thought, but did not go out of the bedroom again for the broom.

In the dusk she could see the woman's hat, small, flat-brimmed, with a tiny flip of veil, but mostly she saw it so much she forgot about it. First she had kept the hat in the valise to let it rankle her if it was going to, but then, when it didn't, she took it out and hung it from the mirror above the bureau before she hid the valise in the fountain.

She turned the light off and lay awake in the bed that was just starting to fit her until she heard the sound of the boys going down the stairs in whatever commotion they thought necessary to seem to be sneaking. She sat up again and leaned in the bed toward the sound of them and waited.

One or the other of them, whichever one was first, dropped a boot down the stairs. She'd be able to tell who it was when he got to the bottom because Junior came onto his right foot with a thud where the last step was shorter than the others and Bobby Joe didn't. At the top of the stairs since he had learned to count, Junior had started with his left foot and ended on the floor with the little surprised thud she heard now. So it was Junior who had dropped the boot and it would be Bobby Joe coming next and hissing at him.

Marilyn lay flat down again on the bed, curling the edges of warmth around her and listening to the puck puck sounds rain was making from the eaves into a still night held down and damp.

She was thinking, in quiet loops that slid away and back, what she had thought on the part of her walk home, that maybe the valise of money Merle had won from the South American fellow should not really have been buried in the cemetery as she had at first thought, that her peace of mind was truly at more peace having the boys know about it than anyone else who could go out with a shovel to the cemetery with no houses nearby and rob graves.

And there was Bobby Joe hissing and moving them out the door, and the house changed with the weight of them going off the floor onto the porch.

With the front door open, she could hear rain from the porch roof drop onto the ferns in soft fuzzy noises, hit more sharply on the wooden step where it fell into a narrow puddle, and on the fountain in the yard where it barely stirred the wet and sticking Easter grass.

She heard Junior sit down on the porch floor to put his feet into the boots and heard Junior splash some words and Bobby Joe say, "You're the one that locked it," and knew he meant the truck where he always left the keys inside hanging from the ignition.

Then they moved off and she could hear light and easy rain fall into quiet night and hit so softly against the house and ground that it made the air more quiet. And she heard from the back of the house, outside her window, a clash like of wire coat hangers where Junior walked his foot into the cardboard wardrobe Bobby Joe had dragged back there and Junior say, "Damn." She could, lying flat in her bed and looking at the ceiling, see them, standing still, Bobby Joe with his arms around Junior to stop him walking through the whole wardrobe, stretching their ears to listen to tell if any of the clashing motion had reached inside. Marilyn lay very still and when she heard the soft clashing motion that would be Bobby Joe, holding Junior back with one hand, reaching into the tangle of wire hangers, she let out her breath, and the next breaths pounded in her ears.

In front of the house, through the open door, she heard Bobby Joe say, "You rolled your window all the way up, right?"

Rain dropped in soft fuzzy balls onto the ferns and sharper chinks onto the puddle on the wooden stair and a door of the truck came open.

Against the rain fuzz on the ceiling, Marilyn watched to see if they were going to start the truck. See if they would drive out to the cemetery at this time of night.

The truck door closed almost closed and came open and closed again, hard. She could hear Bobby Joe and Junior on the lawn, large shapes moving in darkness. After a time, she heard their voices again and a thud of the fountain tire and, "That's all right, then," Marilyn thought. Edges of the bed curled around her. "That's all right. I can keep my eye on it."

T eedie Williams worked as night watchman for the Foley Company keeping an eye on the boilers. What he had to do was check them and make sure the temperature and pressure stayed where they were supposed to and, if they didn't, call the number of the boiler man who would come and shut them down and fix them. Teedie didn't have to fix them himself. He only had to watch them. It didn't take much energy, but it took the time from ten in the evening until six in the morning when he went home to sleep, if he hadn't slept enough during his watch, and to eat something, which he didn't call breakfast, and drink coffee and think about the mink ranch and the money.

He had read an article of information he'd forgotten about minks for a Boy Scout project in nature study or wildlife, and the scoutmaster, who didn't think minks qualified as wildlife living the pampered lives they did, according to Teedie's report, made him do another on birds.

When Teedie was a Boy Scout, Ronnie Bengstad had a Fiftieth Boy Scout Jamboree badge for a jamboree he had never gone to, had bought it for a quarter at a tag sale and wouldn't sell it to Teedie for a dollar—which Teedie thought was a pretty good return on his investment since neither of them could wear it on his uniform anyway. It was just that Teedie wanted it.

Ronnie Bengstad also had a piece of quartz rock with a stripe of something gold running through it that Ronnie said was real gold that Teedie doubted. One time Ronnie swapped a quicksilver dime, slippery in his hands, for Teedie's best shooter marble—that he won with every time —and Teedie found out later, from Oliver Gammon who traded Ronnie for the shooter, that it was an ordinary dime coated with mercury.

In Boy Scouts, Teedie had promised to be clean in thought, word, and deed and so didn't swear, which his mother and uncle and grandmother wouldn't let him do anyway, and behaved himself, mostly.

It wasn't until later, when he no longer lived with his mother and uncle or visited, for days at a time, his grandmother, that he thought he understood what the Boy Scout creed meant by "thought" and why they added it. Later, when his "thought" became just as clear to him and more clear sometimes, especially at night, reading magazines behind the desk they gave him in the maintenance department at Foley's, than his deed, he thought he understood.

What he would do sometimes, before he went to work at ten, was to stop at the Rod and Gun Club for one beer and let some of the atmosphere of the bar cling to him for when he went and sat at the desk.

The night he had off he stayed a little past ten at the Rod and Gun so he was sure Adley Walker-Stanton would be at the desk at Foley and then he walked home and got into bed and opened the magazines.

All right," Marilyn said the next morning, sure as she'd been because of the hat she had found in the valise that Teedie was a woman, "who is this poker player?"

"Teedie Williams?" Junior said. "Lives down behind Jake's package store. See him at the Rod and Gun early."

"Nobody is named Teedie and there's no place down behind Jake's. What does this—man?—do for a living? He doesn't win at poker."

"There's a place there if you're looking for it," Junior said and pulled chords out of the guitar.

The man looked as if he could own a mink farm, and the way he looked at her—starting at her head and dropping to her feet and working his way back up slowly—made her feel like a hooker, and Marilyn thought that's part of it then and changed all the minds that had thought she could come here and meet the man and find out about the money to agree with all the minds that had said it was a damn fool thing to do and the ones that said you don't need to know anyway. If it had been worth anything he would have told you. And though she had bought the nail polish and rouge and blonde wig and nylons, the cotton dress and belt to look like this, specifically so he wouldn't shut the door, Marilyn turned in the yard now so he would shut the door.

She stepped away from him on the path through weeds that stood high on each side of dark flattened earth, on shoes that pinched her toes, and listened carefully to soft birds that called from trees, to a car that pulled up to Jake's in front and turned the engine off, to hear him say, "Wait," if he was going to, "Maybe I can help you."

He didn't say it and her shoulders sagged her breasts back onto her ribs and she lifted her chin and he touched her elbow. "Excuse me, lady. I am very rude. You are such a surprise."

Marilyn stopped stepping forward in the path and, from thinking about walking calmly, normally, around the corner at Jake's, where she had had the boys wait with the truck, she leaped back to her senses in such a rush that her elbow jerked from his touch and she had to turn to him and say, "I'm sorry. You surprised me."

"We are both a surprise, then," he said and, "Will you sit down?" and offered her the path to the small place behind Jake's that she hadn't seen until she was looking for it, and she began steeling herself again for what it must be inside, worse than her own in that it was damp probably, and he held the door.

"Please, will you have a seat? How may I help you?"

Inside the shack was clean, the very few things tidy on shelves, and not as dark as she would have thought, and she thought it was the porch roof that made her house so dark that she kept the door open and sat at the kitchen table on the porch.

"You are Teedie Williams?" Marilyn said, and he indicated a folding wooden chair next to a small table, and she started to sit on the edge of it and thought it would collapse and sat farther back and thought it would tip and lunged herself forward to keep from tipping and coughed to cover her confusion. Teedie unfolded another folding chair from against the wall and set it in front of her and sat in it and said, "I am Teedie, yes. You are looking for me?" His glance slid around the shelves on the walls and across the bed behind her and Marilyn thought to wonder what he might have there that she shouldn't know about now that she knew his name. And then he sat back in the chair and it was all right. Whatever it was was covered.

He was taller sitting than he looked standing and Marilyn sat straight in the chair and held the edges and said, "My husband."

"Yes, yes," he agreed. "It is always the husband."

"What?"

"Excuse me, lady. A joke only. I'm sorry. Your husband?"

"Oh. Yes. Was Merle Benoit."

"Your husband was Merle Benoit. Yes. I am sorry."

Marilyn, who had let her glance fall to his knee where a tear in the jeans fabric had sprouted soft white fur at the edges, looked at his face quickly.

"No, no," Teedie said. "I am sorry about his death I mean. That's all. The man who owned the mink ranch. Several years ago."

She let her glance touch the fur around his knee. "I understand you knew him."

"I knew him. Yes." He shifted his chair backwards a couple of inches by wiggling his hips to move the chair legs one way and then the other.

"You used to play poker."

"Poker. Yes."

"And you lost some money?"

"I have lost money, always, when I play poker."

"Yes," Marilyn said this time. It seemed to her that she had been there a long time or perhaps had been there before or perhaps had known the man before. Teedie had settled his chair where he wanted it and sat in it now as if she had been here before and he was comfortable.

"I have come to ask about the money."

"The money? Oh, no. I always paid. I paid before we left the table, believe me." He was on his feet and standing behind the chair, shorter now with his hands over the top of the back of it, and he was looking at her now the way he had looked, earlier, around the room.

Marilyn let go of the chair and put her hands in front of her, "No, no. I have the money."

"Because I paid. Every time before we left the table."

"How much?"

"Whatever I owed I paid. Right away. No debts. I don't owe."

"No." She stood and brought her hands from trying to calm the air between them to her sides and wished now she had brought, to hold onto, the pocketbook Bobby Joe had said she ought to carry when he and Junior hooted at her on the porch and Bobby Joe said, "Lipstick," and they tipped over, laughing, and Marilyn didn't wait for them to go to the truck, went herself and climbed up the steering wheel and sat in the middle.

"It's all right," she told Teedie, calming herself by saying it. "I mean how much money was it? Altogether? Do you know?"

"How much?"

He gestured to the chair and she let the backs of her knees touch the edge of the seat and she sat in the chair.

Teedie pulled his chair back to where he was standing and set it up and lowered himself into it. He put one ankle across the other knee and slid his shoulder blades down the chair back and to the ceiling said, "Merle Benoit. It was a lot of money over all. I think I figured out one time it was close to six thousand. You have it now?"

"I have it."

Teedie's glance flew around the room. To the ceiling he said, "You have the mink ranch?"

Marilyn stopped turning her head every time a shadow dove over the weeds and looked at his knee, which suddenly looked extremely familiar to her, as if she had done this before, as if she would know exactly what it felt like to touch it if she leaned forward to touch it, and said, "I have it."

Outside the open door shadows flew over the wet green weeds and the path. Teedie made a motion in his chair which brought both feet onto the floor, and Marilyn looked up in time to see a shadow from the weeds expand into the room and Teedie's chair collapse onto itself as Teedie leaped backwards over it. He lifted it in his hands across the front of him as the next shadow expanded into Junior right behind Bobby Joe. And Marilyn, in the first thrust of standing, sat again, fast, hard, on the edge of the seat.

The chair behind her tipped forward and Bobby Joe and Junior, both, with their hands on their hips and still moving forward in the room, ignored her and let the chair crash closed behind her and nip her ankle. Marilyn jumped forward and looked backward at the chair and the boys she had put behind her, and something hard and flat—that she realized as she sat backwards again into the arms now of her two sons who had recovered, if not any grace they should have had, at least their reactions—was the flat of the chair Teedie had swung. Sagging between Junior and Bobby Joe, feeling the slam imprint of the chair across her breasts, she saw Teedie flap open the chair he had used to fend her off and slide it underneath her while Junior and Bobby Joe held her, saw him dive away again out the door, shouting, "Sorry. Sorry. My mistake."

In a silence so sudden it fell like rain around her, Marilyn placed her hands again at the edges of the chair seat.

"Ma," Bobby Joe said, and Junior said, "We didn't know if you were all right."

Marilyn's elbows came unglued from her sides and her feet floated somewhere from the floor in front of her. She glanced around the room and slid off the chair and Junior rolled her onto his shoulder and carried her to the truck in front of Jake's.

He put her in at the passenger door and climbed in and let her slump against him. Bobby Joe got in and started the truck and put it into reverse and let the noise of it fill the cab before backing out.

"Wasn't a good idea, I guess," he said to Junior. "Going in to defend her." He put the truck in first and Marilyn's head rolled on Junior's shoulder. He put his elbow against her chest to hold her against the seat.

"Guess not. How would we know though?"

"Guess it probably won't look to her as if we were out for her own good."

"Nope. Right. Probably going to look to her like we just got tired of twiddling our thumbs, maybe, and Jake's didn't have any comic books and we came in to get her so we could go home."

"Afraid it's going to."

Marilyn could see Teedie down in the road, past the fence posts at the end of the driveway, past the fountain, diving and weaving and trying to see the house without being seen. She could tell it was him because of his height unless it was a little boy which she didn't think so.

She could tell it was him anyway because just seeing him there made her breasts hurt. Casually, since he was far enough away still, she got up from the kitchen table where she had just collected the cards from a solitaire she didn't win, and stepped into the house and ran to her bedroom on the first floor. Pulling the muumuu over her head as she went, she walked nose-first, since her hands and the dress were over her head, into the door jamb where she didn't think it would be and grabbed on the rebound, now that the dress was above her eyes, for the cotton dress she had bought and the wig from the top drawer and the lipstick which leaped away from her fingers as she scrabbled for it first on the bureau top and then in the dust on the floor beneath it.

"Hello," Teedie called from the porch. "Hello."

Marilyn tied the belt and dabbed baby powder over her nose and called, "Just a minute," while Teedie on the porch made sure the truck was not just parked somewhere he hadn't seen it. He let his shoulders down to rest his elbows on his waist and to tuck against his chest the bunch of flowers that he hoped didn't look as if he'd gone out of his way to pick from Jeannetta Tillotson's flowering garden on the way.

He looked over the porch railing and across the driveway downhill to the barn, trying to calculate if it was one or two floors of minks or if they lined up in wire mesh boxes the way they showed off rabbits at the fair and how much trouble it was keeping them anyway.

"And why aren't they outside on a day as nice as this?"

"Something about the sunlight streaking their fur," Marilyn said behind him, and he turned to see her looking the same as she had at his place—once he remembered what she had looked like there since he hadn't thought to remember ahead of time—except for a very white nose that looked dipped in flour, and realized he had spoken his thought out loud.

"Are they much trouble?" he said and extended his elbow from his waist which brought the bouquet into her reach.

"Thank you," Marilyn said and stood the flowers into the glass of iced tea she had been drinking playing solitaire and put her face into them to sniff and came away with a very red nose where the white one had been.

Teedie immediately thought he had hit her there with the chair and felt badly all over again so that when he said, "I came to apologize. I'm sorry," he sounded quite sincere. He had just remembered, for sure, slamming her breasts and not her nose, when Marilyn said, "No. They're really no trouble at all. Not anything like you'd imagine." And it took him a minute to realize she meant the minks he had asked about and not her breasts.

He looked so much more forlorn for remembering the minks in place of the breasts that Marilyn offered him a glass of iced tea and waved him to the kitchen table.

Teedie remembered the truck and looked over his shoulder to see if it were jouncing, as he suspected, into the driveway with both the boys out the windows ready to pound him, and Marilyn went inside, and the driveway stayed empty.

Teedie was rolling around in his head, while he shuffled the cards from one hand to the other, for the appropriate comment to make about the lawn statuary in the form of a painted rubber tire fountain with Easter grass and Christmas ornaments, since it wasn't something meant to be ignored. But what he said when she came out with two glasses of iced tea was what he had really come to say, "Do you still have it?"

That he was looking, as she handed him the iced tea, at her breasts where he had whacked her—so as not to stare at her nose which had turned again alarming white—made Marilyn think he was asking the indecent question her sons must have thought he was asking earlier. She looked past the fountain hoping for the truck to skid into the driveway with the boys climbing out to defend her.

When the iced tea glass stopped coming toward him, Teedie glanced up to see that perhaps he had not made himself clear and said, "Do you still have the valise?"

"The what?"

He didn't know whether to duck or keep reaching his hand for the tea glass and said quickly, "Because, you see, if you have the money and the valise, I would be willing to redeem it, if you're interested."

The tea glass came to rest on the table top in front of him. "Why?"

"It is an embarrassment. The money which I lost to Merle Benoit was my inheritance, part of my inheritance. How would I know he would be such a good gambler?"

"I could have told you," she said and sat at the table across from him and picked up the cards he dealt across to her in his fidgeting.

"And it seems now I have had word that my uncle and my mother may be coming from my country for a visit to see this wonderful place I am living... five card draw," he picked up his cards, "and I have none of the money which I would like to be able to have them see, perhaps in a valise that I have kept safe."

He put down two cards and looked up to see what she would do. Marilyn put down two cards and picked up the two he gave her and laid down her hand to show a pair of threes.

"Just one moment. Just one moment, please. No one has bid."

"I don't know how to play."

"Don't you? At all?"

"Blackjack," she said.

"Blackjack, then." He slid the deck of cards to her. She shuffled and set them down and he cut them into three stacks, which she stacked, and flipped the top card at him and he nodded and she buried it.

"Wait," he said. "Wait. This time before the deal. What are we betting?"

"What do you bet?"

"I have already lost my inheritance. You have it, I think?"

"I think so, yes." Marilyn tried not to flick her glance at the fountain—which she thought she knew the boys had, in their jolting and noisy backings and forthings—deconstructed and reconstructed around the money.

Teedie turned and looked over his shoulder to see that it was not the boys hanging out of the truck that she was watching for. "You have it safely somewhere and I will not ask you to get it out now. You tell me you have it. It is enough."

He looked back across the table at Marilyn, at the white nose which looked clumsily attached to the rest of her face and rubbed his own nose and face and the grin into his chin and when he could, said, "Yes. I will bet U.S. money for the money you have, which is of no value to you anyway and maybe would just save my face in front of my family." His face twitched again and he rubbed and composed it. "I have not the six hundred dollars to bet against your. . ."

"Six thousand," Marilyn said.

"In those times, maybe yes. But we know now, the value of foreign currency has changed very much since then and has, after all, no use to you since no bank here would change it. Perhaps I will become lucky and win it from you before I lose all the U.S. currency I have and become a pauper to the extent that my family will learn I do not own, in actuality, a mink ranch."

"A. . . mink. . . ranch?"

"Which I may have exaggerated to them slightly in the time I was writing, they were that far away and me hoping to win anyway from your husband."

"A mink ranch?" Marilyn folded her hand over the deck of cards and pulled it to her. "What kind of a mink ranch?"

He looked at the spot on the table where the deck of cards had been and puckered his face to let her know how sorry he felt that it was her husband, now dead, who not only hadn't lost the mink ranch to him but had, in further injury, won from him an inheritance which may have been worth anything then and could in fact be worth anything now. He had no idea.

"I only ever played poker with Merle," Teedie said, "because of the mink ranch, you see. I don't generally gamble at all. But maybe I won't lose everything I own before they get here. I understand I have two weeks to produce the money."

Marilyn couldn't remember later for sure whether in his sympathy to express himself about hitting her with the chair he had really touched her breasts, brushing them with his hands, or whether he had just looked at them so much in the afternoon that the accumulation of his looking felt like a caress. Or whether she was just looking for the sympathy she would have liked to have. She remembered his standing, leaning toward her when the truck actually did come careening around the road fence posts into the driveway the way they had both pictured it with the boys—when they saw who it was on the porch—dropping out on either side of it while it was practically still running, churning dust up from the driveway with the doors open. Then Teedie leaped past her, saying, "You owe me half," and ran through the open doorway and through the house and out the back door which he found after running first into the bedroom with the baby powder on the floor and the hat on the mirror and then through the kitchen. Outside the back door at the clothesline and the refrigerator and sofa he could see the boys down by the barn waving their arms and could realize he hadn't heard them behind him and turn and slam past her once again, Marilyn, on the porch with the baby powder from her nose now on her dress front and call, "Three hundred dollars," and dive through the space on the railing and past the truck and sprint down the driveway past the road fence posts, before Bobby Joe and Junior came back up the driveway and saw the baby powder from her nose across the front of her and stopped.

Marilyn turned over the top card from the deck and held it up toward them and they had no idea what she meant and backed off to close the truck doors.

"What's it mean—a three of clubs?"

"Oh. It's just a bluff. She doesn't know either."

And now she would have to go through the fountain one more time for the half of the fortune she had lost unless she somehow won it back if he came again and would play again for the other half.

Half against half more of his own money now.

She knew how to find him and would find him now again, past Jake's, down the path, through the weeds, if he didn't come back for the rest of the money—not only to try to win back from him what she had lost so as not to have to take the fountain apart for it, but to see if he really had touched her where she hurt so hard.

"I'm playing solitaire," she said. "Because when I lose I don't have to pay you any money."

Teedie stood outside the broken-apart piece of railing, holding with one hand the bouquet and tendrils of a pole bean plant from Jeannetta Tillotson's garden, and with one foot drawing a slow arc in the dust of the driveway.

She had seen him this time in time to duck inside, pull on the wig and put the belt around the dress she already had on, catch the lipstick in its flurried leap across the bureau, and pick up the hand of cards before he came past the fountain.

"What am I going to tell my boys this time, am I, when they ask me what you're doing here?"

Teedie stopped drawing his foot across the dust and stepped up to the dattered ferns and looked at each end of the porch railing where it had broken away.

"All right, then," Marilyn said and went inside and wedged the hammer out from under the green uphol-stered chair and laid it on the kitchen table. "You're fixing the porch railing. That's what it'll cost you to cut into this game. It's your deal if I remember." She took the flowers and put them in the tea and went inside to make more so he could come around up the stairs and shuffle the cards and have her cut.

When the truck started around the corner with the sheriff license plate in the window and Junior in the back standing and thudding his hands down onto the roof of the cab and singing the words if not the tune to, "I Gave the Phone My Nickel but It Didn't Give Me You," Teedie leaped backwards from the table with the hammer and broke out the next two sets of rails.

Unless it was raining hard, thumping on the house and the porch roof, battering the ferns and the driveway and tired yard, gushing out the end of gutter on the barn and hitting against the metal downspout where it had come undone and hung crooked against the corner of the barn above the rain barrel, Merle's and Marilyn's seemed quiet.

The barn was far enough from the house and down a little, at the end of the driveway, that Teedie, sitting at the kitchen table on the porch and looking through the window to inside the house where sunlight fell across the room, could think he wouldn't hear the minks anyway. Unless they were in wire cages that they racketed or were spinning wheels the way hamsters or something else had wheels to exercise themselves or unless they weren't in cages and were able to leap around a lot and make thumps on the floorboards, he wouldn't hear them.

Merle hadn't ever wanted to talk to him about the ranch or the minks and Marilyn would only say, "They're not much trouble."

Through the window Teedie could see where sunlight ran across the lap of the green upholstered chair and across something dark on the carpet—that he thought with a thrill could have been old blood.

Teedie looked through the window and began thinking, then that is where she murdered Merle. Right there, when she discovered the woman's hat in the valise. If he had remembered his mother's hat in the valise when he had brought the valise the last time for Merle to win from him, he would have taken it out. But he'd seen it every time he opened the valise for the money he lost, and it had become so familiar that he no longer saw it and the last time, he didn't open the valise at all since there was no money he had to count out.

Right there she had murdered him with a butcher knife probably—Teedie's heart stopped beating and then went thundering on—which was why Teedie hadn't sidled himself up there onto the porch again, once that Merle was gone, and asked Marilyn didn't she need some help now that Merle wasn't there. Because of the hat and the murder and, of course, the two almost full-grown boys.

Teedie shifted the cards from one hand to another and remembered a chair like that his grandmother had had in Queens when he was a boy. A chair that hugged him, when he sat in it, the way his grandmother hugged him in her lap when she told him stories about the old country and how in it he would be a prince had his family stayed— had his grandfather stayed instead of coming here to make his fortune.

Flowers in the iced tea glass were nasturtiums.

"You deal for me," Teedie said, one hand sliding the deck with the jack and the ace he had just turned over across the table to Marilyn while the other hand, under the table, made small circles on Marilyn's knee in the place below the hem of her dress above the tops of her knee-high stockings where when she sat there was bare skin.

His hand, which had first brushed to her knee as if brushing something off his knee, moved in a circle and then one finger made the circles, lightly.

Inside the house, they could hear Junior drop down the stairs and thud the short step at the bottom, and Teedie brushed his hand across Marilyn's knee and brought it above the table to hold his cards, and he sat straight to look at them and say, "Hit me," as Junior came out the door with a rolled comic book.

"What?" Junior said.

"He wants another card," Marilyn told him and slid him the one from the top of the deck.

Junior looked across the yard where Bobby Joe had parked the truck facing the house so as not to rouse the curiosity of anybody sitting on the porch concerning what was under the drop cloth tarp in the back.

He looked down toward the barn. He couldn't hear any of what Bobby Joe was doing, if he was doing anything, moving paint cans around, stacking them to clear a space.

He hooked a chair away from the wall and pulled it beneath him and sat in it and leaned it back against the clapboards and unrolled the comic book.

Teedie and Marilyn flipped the cards onto the table. From the barn was the sound of metallic thunder and the barn doors exploded open and hurled Bobby Joe, with his arms crossed above his head, out into sunlight where his shadow burnt onto the yard. Then, in the same motion it took him to stop his momentum, he was leaping back to the barn doorsill and grabbing the doors to pull them in with him.

The brief action—which had caused Marilyn and Teedie and Junior not to move, but to stop what little motion they were making long enough to turn their heads to the barn and back, and then continue moving cards—created greater stillness and greater quiet. Into it Junior said, "Feisty critters," and Teedie threw down an ace and jack which didn't get him the deal since Marilyn was already dealing for him, but he took the pack of cards, anyway.

"What were you trying to do, stack them to the ceiling? What we ought to do is take them right on outta here why don't we?" Junior said to Bobby Joe while Teedie put a couple nails in the part of the porch railing he was repairing. Marilyn went into the kitchen and Teedie stepped inside.

Teedie might have been surprised, when Junior, not seeing Teedie or Marilyn on the porch, motioned Bobby Joe to back the truck into the barn over the granite doorsill through the open doors so he could shut them and they could unload the bottles, that he didn't see the feisty critters if they were not in cages, come boiling and tearing in a surge out the barn doors or, had they been in cages, didn't hear them rucker up and down and around the sides clashing any exercise wheels.

But Teedie stepped across the open doorsill onto the carpet full of yard dust and crossed to the upholstered chair and sat down, and the crash of its weight, tipping backwards over the broken leg, unsupported by the hammer he'd been using on the porch rail, and the surprise of sliding headfirst into the wall, captured his attention.

On his back, half out of the chair against the wall, with his eyes closed and seeing fireflies against the dark inside them, Teedie was thinking in very fast motion of his bare knees in shorts in the summertime at his grandmother's in the cool green of her apartment above the ground with tomato plants and parsley in the windows. It was something he hadn't remembered since he had grown into a teenager and at sixteen, left school and home and his grandmother's all in the same day with the clothes he was wearing and a hat of his mother's that she no longer wore and didn't know he had, and the valise of his grandfather's containing the pink paper money his grandmother called their fortune from the old country, the fortune that at sixteen he thought of as his as the last of the family.

He hadn't remembered before being the little boy because he didn't know how to remember past being the teenager, who, while his grandmother fixed him lunch that day went to the stowaway closet under the eaves and took out the valise and stood it outside her apartment door and while he ate the lunch worried if it would still be there or if he should have waited, and after he kissed her good-bye in the kitchen while she had her hands in suds and dishwater, took the valise that still stood there and moved far enough north to get a job and find the place behind Jake's and stay for thirty years that didn't seem like much.

What had made him stop and stay was the mink ranch and his thought that some way he could perhaps do something about minks.

From thinking about the little boy with bare knees and the first time he had seen the mink ranch sign, Merle's and Marilyn's—when it had been just Merle sitting on the porch swing made from the old frame spring of a twin bed and Teedie asked him for a job working on the ranch, and Merle refused, saying it was a one-man operation—Teedie started thinking, in the flash of a moment, about the years he had spent as night watchman at Foley's.

His knees were bent over the edge of the seat of the chair upturned toward the ceiling and, from thinking about a wash of nights in which heat and rain and icy snow mixed to land him at his door by morning, Teedie looked past the soft sprout of white fur at the knee on his jeans to see Marilyn with the two glasses of iced tea held away from her sides at shoulder height, stopped on the dark stains on the carpet, which he didn't know had been made by oil from Junior's Norton when he'd had it inside in the winter.

Before he rolled away from the wall and brought his knees to his chest beside the chair and pushed off the carpet to stand, Teedie closed his eyes for a moment, for the length of time of the job as night watchman in one of those years, and watched the fireflies in fast motion inside his eyelids.

What he didn't tell Marilyn, then, was that it hadn't been his mother and his uncle who had informed him that they would like, within two weeks, the return of the fortune in foreign dollars, and it wasn't his mother and uncle he expected to collect it.

Bobby Joe wasn't telling Junior what he knew about the Norton 750 which was that it was gone in flames crashed against a tree that had the bark and leaves seared off one side and a piece of metal embedded in the trunk. He thought it would make Junior feel worse to know it was gone rather than better to know he hadn't been riding it. Bobby Joe didn't know himself whether he believed the Norton would have run into the tree no matter who was on it, and if he told Junior, Junior might just convince him that if Bobby Joe hadn't sold it for the truck, and if Junior'd been driving it, he and the Norton would both have been safe.

Bobby Joe, consequently, didn't know if he should feel like the hero for saving Junior's life or keep feeling like the bad guy for ruining it. What he did know was that earning what he earned working part-time at Jake's package store was not going to accumulate for him enough money to replace the old Norton with any kind of other Norton.

He had a hundred dollars on it with the dealer not to sell it, but when the dealer, with sand in his elbows, crawled from under the charred tree, he folded the business and left with the money.

"I don't care if you've got any use for them," Jake said about the empty bottles he had in cardboard cartons in the back room where he put them when people brought them back and there was no deposit. "You take them. Take them to the dump or for target practice I don't care. Just get them out of here."

That was when Bobby Joe put on the Davy Crockett hat and loaded the cartons of empty whiskey and gin and wine bottles into the back of the truck and drove them home, moved the paint cans, and unloaded the bottles, with the labels still on them, into the barn.

Later, he couldn't remember if it was before or because of the bottles that he got the good idea about how to get Junior another Norton 750.

If he and Marilyn hadn't been so mad about Junior's driving the motorcycle through the porch railing and if they hadn't been wondering whether what he would do next was drive it up the stairway, Bobby Joe wouldn't have taken the Norton to sell in the first place. And if the dealer, who had about four used motorcycles and a bunch of parts on order hadn't said to Bobby Joe when he saw him looking at the truck, the only tall thing in the yard, "That's mine. I drive it. It's not for sale," Bobby Joe wouldn't have traded the Norton, would have sold it flat and continued to walk to work.

When he lost the bike, Junior refused to walk or let Bobby Joe drive him and flat out quit his job making ball bearings at Foley's manufacturing company. He took up guitar-singing which he could do outside on the front porch when the weather was nice and inside next to the oil stove named Florence when the weather turned cold.

"You know what that thing is we always thought was a water tank for watering the minks?" Bobby Joe said. "You know what that is?"

"Yeah, It's a watering tank without a place at the bottom for the water to go into a trough."

"Yeah, all right. But if it is, how come he didn't leave it down at the barn, how come he brought it up here behind the house with the oil tanks? And if there aren't any minks, how come we need one even?"

Junior shrugged his shoulders.

Bobby Joe felt really good about putting two and two together. He felt when he did it that he had discovered some treasure.

"All right," he said. "You know that diagram penciled onto the barn wall back of that little stone fireplace with the hollow in the top just the right size to fit the water tank into?"

The second time Marilyn saw the inside of the barn, she looked to see how the cat got in and found the square hole above the sill behind the rain barrel and this time opened the doors to go inside. This time what surprised her wasn't the lack of minks, which she went into the barn expecting not to find, and it wasn't the canvases which she thought would be right where they were all down the side in front of the window and across the back windows and the one in front. What surprised her was what was against the other wall, the wall without windows where Merle had rigged some sort of metal pieces going into and out of each other with what looked like a water tank in the middle sitting in a small stone fireplace built onto a piece of granite hearth with the flue hooked into a length and crook of rusted stovepipe out the back barn wall.

So when the insurance salesman got out of a green car in the driveway and Merle, from lying on the porch swing with his arms crossed over his chest asleep, stood up full-length in one smooth motion to the porch railing, Marilyn was thinking that this time, because of the important equipment in the barn and the possibility of fire, Merle would not hold his arm out over the railing with his finger down and turning in a circle to indicate the man was to turn around and keep going.

The man, this time, didn't try to get his foot onto the porch step or start talking even. He made a circle around his car and swung his briefcase and himself inside through the door he'd come out of and waved and Merle was already back on the porch swing full-length, asleep with his arms crossed over his chest.

"Course we could afford it," Merle said when he woke up. "It's a damned nuisance. Insures against all the things that'll never happen. You'll see. And won't insure upon acts of God. And you can bet that anything strikes here or the barn would be an act of God, you bet. Flood, tornado, hail, lightning, fire. And then investigations. You don't think they'd want to investigate every bit of this property before they insured it?"

When Marilyn put up the fountain after Merle's death and rolled the water tank up behind the house to stand with the refrigerator and the oil tank, it was because she pictured them—people coming to investigate the house and barn. She saw them in the house first, looking through closets and bureaus and kitchen cupboards and finding, where she had wedged it under the headboard of the bed, the valise with Merle's poker winnings which he had shown her the outside of the night he had won all there was to win from a foreigner, Teedie something, playing cards in the kitchen at the Rod and Gun Club.

She had brought the valise first thing from the barn where she pictured them looking next, looking, through all the canvases and metal connected parts, for the minks and finding the valise near the back wall where she found it, behind canvases, hanging from a beam by a rope which she could untie from a coat hook pounded into the wall, to lower the valise.

She thought of the fountain because, hanging in the barn where investigators would find it first thing and arrest her probably for counterfeiting, the valise did not seem connected to the barn or house, really. So she decided the thing was to have a less visible place, free from either where she could keep her eye on it.

And then, when Bobby Joe brought tires for the fountain, driving them up in the junkyard pickup without doors or a tailgate, tickled that Bosco had given him the sheriff license tag, and when he brought two tires of each size instead of one, then she had the idea of putting up the fountain at the cemetery, not to put the valise into, but to mislead investigators going through the house if they wondered.

Bobby Joe and Junior constructed the fountain, gluing tires together after they were cut and painted, using caulking which, the night it was finished, Marilyn unstuck around the middle tire and restuck, cementing the valise full of foreign money inside.

So this time, having learned that again she didn't want to know what was in the barn, she deliberately didn't notice, when she hung out clothes, that the water tank that she had rolled through weeds behind the house was gone from next to the refrigerator, leaving a white, lush, perfectly round spot on the grass and weeds.

And she didn't hear any loud snaps of metal to speak of sitting where she sat to deal out the cards on the porch.

"You know that diagram in the barn on the wallboards done in lead pencil?" Bobby Joe said, and Junior said, "Yeah. The one where you said Daddy was designing a new reaper or something."

"All right. Listen. What if it isn't a reaper?"

"Then it's some other contraption. So what?"

It wasn't until Bobby Joe was unloading the cartons off the back of the truck into the barn that he thought to remember something about bottles. Something, he slid a carton across the barn floorboards, about bottles, and, he thought, metal pieces, and a ladder, and light coming in on the side from a dusty window.

He moved the cartons again from where he'd put them on the floorboards and located the iron ring in the floor that once he thought was for tying something so it wouldn't get away.

It wasn't that Marilyn suddenly gave Junior and him permission to go down to the barn now. But Marilyn only went down to the barn a few times and then stopped. And Bobby Joe worked himself into worrying that the minks, which he still thought were there, would be dying without care. Merle had spent so much time down there. And his fear of the minks' dying reached a point greater than his fear of Marilyn's telling him to stay out of there. So to take care of Marilyn and save the minks from starvation, he opened the barn doors, which were never locked, in the middle of a morning, and came out years older and walked to town for his first job weeding Jeannetta Tillotson's garden.

"You know that metal—when I found it you said, 'Too bad we didn't have this when we were making go-carts.' "

"In the barn? Underneath?" Junior said.

"All right. You know those glass bottles we wanted to know what were doing there?"

Junior shook his head.

"That's 'cause you were only thinking go-carts. All right. What you have right here on the wall is a diagram for putting together a whiskey still. And what you have under your feet there where somebody hid 'em after Merle died, is all the metal pieces you need to do it except the watering tank that is standing up against the refrigerator and the gas tanks behind the house."

"And what you don't have," Junior said, "is any idea how to make it."

"Well, yeah. But that's got to be easy. The hard part is done, right? Getting all the metal and figuring out how it goes together. That's all here. Don't worry. I'll figure out how to make it."

"Yeah, well, you put it right here though, you're going to be right in the middle of that fireplace thing is where you're going to land."

"All right. I haven't figured that out yet. But maybe you have to heat it. Cook it or something. Look if you look here," he put his thumb on the board where the broad pencil marks cut into the wood. "Doesn't it look sort of like where the stovepipe goes up? I think that's part of it. That's all right," Bobby Joe told him. "I'm working on it. There's a lot of stuff that doesn't make sense. If you don't know, for instance, what the tooth-brush is, which I haven't figured out, taking the toothbrush and plunging it up and down in the beer doesn't make any sense."

"I didn't know you needed beer to make whiskey."

"Well, yeah, one of the things you need, I'm finding out, is beer that you run through."

"I thought it was corn, sprouted and unsprouted."

"That, too. All right. I'm still working on it. What it is, is you can't ask anybody, see, and not have them suspicion what we're doing."

"We're not doing anything that I can see."

"What we're going to be doing."

Bobby Joe couldn't figure out whether he was a hero or stupid for trying to replace Junior's Norton. He figured he was stupid for saying anything to Junior about the still since Junior never went down to the barn anyway and, except for the noise, would never have discovered the still.

"All right."

Bam. Bobby Joe's eyelashes hit his eyebrows and his eyes stayed open, glaring at the ceiling. Lying flat on the top of the bed on top of the clothes and hangers he had pulled out of the wardrobe before he hurled it out the window, he started to wonder if Jake had given him the bottles on purpose, because he knew something about the still, had maybe known about it when Merle was running, had maybe . . .

And was it good because if he wanted to, Jake had the way to distribute, say, any liquor he wanted or was it a trap, say, that if he once got going again Jake was looking to turn him in . . . because Jake hadn't said anything about bottles to him before, about taking them to the dump or home if he could use them until . . . Of course, he didn't have the truck then either, and it might have been that, that now that he had the truck he could move the bottles . . . Or did he think, maybe, that now that he had the truck to move the bottles and whatever else he needed to move to transport . . .

Bobby Joe turned on the flashlight from next to the bed and felt under the bed for the composition notebook he had found with the bottles in the small room under the barn and read again his father's directions and records and comments in brown ink about what worked and what beaded and when and how much. And he tried again to puzzle out whatever was there with whatever he had to guess that his father would have known and not thought necessary to tell him.

Bobby Joe couldn't know then, how looking into the clear water in the cellar had started Merle thinking about his own grandfather running whiskey on the mountain where a brook went down past the laurel bushes and under pine trees and how he knew right then, if he could find the old man's cabin, just find it at the end of a dirt driveway he almost remembered, that he—probably with his eyes closed because they had gone there so many times after dark, before he even knew what they were doing, before he thought to wonder—could find the still.

But what he didn't know was whether it would still be there or if someone else had had the idea before him. And what he didn't count on was its being that grown up with trees, brush, where space had used to be open to the sky. His grandfather had gone into the woods in different places so as not to wear a path. Merle stood at the foot of the porch stairs at his grandfather's where laurels had grown above the railings of the front porch and shaded the windows and the porch floor, littered with chips of pine cones that critters had gnawed and rolled around and the dead brown blossoms of the laurels and the dead brown needles of the pines, and turned around.

Hot dry air pressed him between the laurels and with sunlight on the backs of his hands Merle tried to feel the night.

He moved to the right and ducked around the corner of the cabin where leaves, sticky with sunshine, filled what had used to be space between the cabin and the woods. He knew where he should hear the stream and cut through ferns to its dry bed and stood in the quiet where stones on the bottom of the dry bed looked like stones in the floor of the cellar when it was dry. Merle walked up the dry stream bed and where the laurels broke into pine trees, three in a row, he left the stream bed and crossed the fallen brown pine needles. It wouldn't be far from the stream bed, just far enough that a trough, bringing water ... He saw it, old, what looked like a fort kids might have made with cut-down trees and the dead tops of them across the top, the old dead needles, the logs looking somehow dusty out of dryness, with one corner sunken onto itself and the whole thing somehow less big than he remembered it, somehow dried out.

To move the pieces downhill to the cabin took him several trips and he didn't bother to hide his trail, followed the dry creek bed to the three pines and loaded up and carried downhill the pieces he was laying under the tarp in the back of the truck.

Under the tarp with them he put the piece end of lumber he'd brought and drawn on with the stub end of pencil, a picture of the still and a label for each part.

Without the still, the inside of the shelter sloped to the collapsed corner and Merle walked down the dry bed one more time and climbed into the truck.

We need water," Bobby Joe said. "The one thing that has me stopped now. All right. You see," Bobby Joe put his thumb onto the diagram, "this barrel has what is called a worm—a condenser." He pointed at the spiral in the barrel and with his thumb on the barrel, then he did know how. Suddenly he did remember the time when they were kids that they followed a cat to the square hole cut in the siding of the barn and leaned themselves down to see if they could fit in, if Bobby Joe could, since he was smaller, and got themselves muddy with squishing the grass and earth there where water in just a trickle from the end of a pipe sogged the ground that smelled like sour root beer or sarsaparilla until Merle whupped them both for being near the barn and maybe disturbing the minks.

And then he did know how, if he moved the wooden barrel, held together by iron hoops, from under the corner of the roof into the place where the trapdoor lifted and set it down onto the platform for it, it would be the right height to catch the water running downhill from the cellar. And, if, for instance, he took the leftover piece of pipe and fitted it over the end of the pipe he would still find where the ground was soggy when the cellar was full, it would be the right height to drop into the barrel and cool the steam in the worm and then run off through the pipe Merle had dug into a trench to go out past the back corner of the barn to run off through the laurel.

"Well, that's it," he said to Junior. Bobby Joe felt real good when he put two and two together.

And then Bobby Joe started looking backwards, looking for something, a sign maybe to let him know whether, if he was going to do this, he ought to drive up to the farmer's regional market for corn. If he did how would he keep it until the cellar filled? Did it only fill in the springtime or was it in the fall, too? He couldn't remember, hadn't noticed, and wouldn't ask Marilyn. What if she didn't know about that either, the way she hadn't known about the minks. Or if somewhere nearby, there was someone who grew corn and was just looking to sell nine bushels, dried so he could sprout what he had to sprout of it to start to make what the notebook called beer.

J unior left the house by walking straight across the doorsill and porch floorboards, down the step, not looking over at Marilyn or Bobby Joe to say good-night so Bobby Joe could grin at the way he'd wet and combed his hair or buttoned the cuffs on his shirt, looking straight ahead to the end of the driveway where he was going to turn toward the Rod and Gun Club, and then the truck door slammed beside him. Without meaning to look, he turned and Bobby Joe said, "Hey," coming at him with a small canister like an aerosol can aimed at him with a little blue horn on top.

Junior jumped back and put his hands in front of him and stopped walking.

"Look at this," Bobby Joe said.

"What is it?" He looked at the aerosol can, white with writing, and a blue plastic horn on the top that looked like the kind of horn they used to have on a tricycle he remembered, but that horn had a bulb on the end to squeeze noise through.

"It's a boat horn." Bobby Joe put it into Junior's hand. "Yeah."

"That's what it's called. A boat horn."

Junior turned it around in his hands and put his thumb on the button on top of the blue horn.

Bobby Joe took it back from him. "That sets it off. You don't want to set it off."

Junior waited. Now that Bobby Joe had taken it away from him, he didn't know what to do with his hands which seemed very large and obvious to him coming out from his buttoned cuffs. "What does it do if you set it off?"

Bobby Joe turned it around in his hands. "Makes a loud noise. A very loud noise." He aimed it at the barn and punched the button down with his thumb and a short blast of very loud boat horn hit the side of the barn, and Marilyn on the porch dropped the ace she was placing for solitaire.

"You wouldn't want to have that go off in the house, now, would you?"

"Can't say as I would," Junior said. "What's it for?"

"It's for people with boats who are lost in the fog so somebody could find them or to let somebody else know they're there and not ram into them if they don't see them coming. But, listen. Guy at the hardware said people are using them for defense."

Junior shoved his hands into his pockets and let his thumbs stay out and waited.

"Well, don't you see? If you had somebody come up on your porch, say, that you didn't want them there or they didn't leave when you wanted them to and your sons were working down in the barn, say, and they didn't know that he was even here, maybe, because he always walks up the driveway, well, then, a short blast on this and we'd come running."

Junior looked past the porch railing at Marilyn sitting at the kitchen table and at the tea glass full of flowers. Marilyn picked up the piles of cards and made a deck and shuffled.

"Or even if we weren't here," Bobby Joe said, "would you want to hang around with that blasting? If you held it down? In the house?"

"A boat horn," Junior said and backed away.

Bobby Joe grinned and aimed it at him.

"Don't you know better than to aim a loaded gun?" Junior said.

"They're all loaded," Bobby Joe said. "I'm going to keep it on the table there. Just so's we all know."

When he first walked into the Rod and Gun, Candy wasn't there, leaning against the bar where the girls filled their trays and dropped cherries into the drinks. With his foot, Junior hooked a stool at the bar and pulled it underneath him and rested his elbows against the edge of the bar as if he had a comic book held there and waited for the beer to appear on the pages between his elbows.

He didn't see why Bobby Joe thought making liquor and selling it was going to get them money to buy his Norton when anyone in Cedar Brake could walk into the Rod and Gun and order the kind of beer he liked.

Music from the jukebox pounded around the ceiling and a ceiling fan pushed smoke and music back down into the voice and noise of the room.

Junior turned on the stool and raised his hand at people he knew, mostly from being in high school with them. If he thought about it at all, they had been just the same in high school as they were in the bar, making paper balls out of the straw papers and throwing them, leaning on tables with their elbows, and Jamie Edmondson ready to stand up and push the table back at Ready Ferris partway through the night and wave his fists at him and holler, "Sit down, then, you don't want to fight," and let the fan push the music and smoke down.

At the end of the bar, Candy leaned against the backs of the two waitresses and said something that made them laugh. Junior watched to see if she looked for him, because he couldn't hear anything except music and noise, doubled by reflection in the bar mirror behind the rows of bottles with little plastic spouts where he couldn't see himself. But she didn't, and turned away from the bar, and he looked at the beer between his elbows.

The Guys and Dolls rooms at the Rod and Gun Club were side by side out the door labeled Restrooms. After he'd drunk four beers while watching Candy finish dancing on the tiny stage in one corner to whatever songs throbbed on the jukebox, Junior slid off the bar stool and over to the restroom door which he pushed open, thinking in a rather fuddled and tired and discouraged way about what it might take to have Candy dancing with him, and walked, almost, right into her on the other side of the door and overcame his surprise just in time to walk her against the smooth wall opposite the Guys and Dolls doors and lean her there with his knee against the wall.

She was wearing some sort of jangles, he couldn't exactly tell what but something that jittered when he did, that, when he leaned against her, clashed as she moved her arms, and he saw then it was a bracelet, hung with coins or some sort of metal discs, coins he thought, that made noise as she moved her arms. He let go of her waist, caught hold of her arms instead, and the jangle was quiet. She let him move his mouth against hers, but when he stopped, she twisted and wiggled out of his grasp, and the coins clashed again, and she slid along the wall and left his weight against it. He hung on for a moment before rolling over and pushing off to go out through the barroom door that had closed behind her.

Then he remembered and turned around and pushed, instead, through the doorway labeled Guys.

On the way out through the barroom, Junior looked for her at the waitress station, and she was looking for him to come out the restroom door. When he did, she turned her chin into the air which made him feel good so he kept going out the door, instead of getting another beer, and started to walk home.

He was feeling some good. He wanted to make noise. He wanted to turn on the Norton and run it up and down the driveway a few times, leaning and sliding to turn it around at the end and come back and shoot, then, after a few times, out past the fountain and past the fence posts onto the summer road clingy with damp from that time of night.

He came into the quiet quiet driveway, and he remembered the tricycle they had had when they were kids, tearing up and down the driveway, beating their legs up and down with the pedals and skidding, and how one time he had taken out the two screws that held the little plastic horn clamped to the handlebars, and while Bobby Joe was having his nap in the room with the brown window shade pulled down to the green part, had blasted it next to the bed.

Marilyn lay in bed looking at the ceiling which she couldn't really see in the dark and told herself not to think of Teedie touching her breasts, if he had or hadn't, and began thinking of Teedie touching her breasts where they still hurt some from the slam of the chair, lifting them with the backs of his hands, his knuckles pressed against them and his thumb crossing the tips of them gently, just gently, like a tongue. And she pictured Teedie the way he looked, sorry he'd hurt her, and saw the little frayed place on his knee which somehow made her like him for being clean and unmended.

She lay on her back because lying on her front, her breasts felt as they had felt when her milk came in with Junior and again with Bobby Joe. She thought of Teedie holding the flowers at his waist, and suddenly what was in front of him was a white and blue boat horn. The sound of it first arched her back as she leaned against him and then made her leap, faster than she could think, to her feet, to stand beside the bed where the sound that had now finished pounded waves around her and thunder and rain through her head. The thought of Teedie, slick and wet in the rain, shivered through her, made her weak, made her lean against the bed and fall back onto it to subside with the afterwaves of the boat horn beating silence and the ceiling.

T he reason Marilyn had for not wanting the dark-uniformed sheriff and officer on her porch with afternoon sun of a perfect day brittle behind them had nothing to do with the valise of foreign money they had traced to Teedie Williams, who had been sitting on the kitchen table with his feet on the part of the porch railing he had fixed.

It had to do with that she might have murdered Merle. At times she still dreamed she could have, in some mad moment, come up behind him in the green upholstered chair in the living room, could have slid along the wall and brought down hard on his head, not the hammer, which was under the chair propping the leg, but some other heavy object, and then could have covered what she had done with one of the crazy Davy Crockett hats he had bought at a flea market and kept in a box up-attic and pretended were mink.

When she was passionate with a hatred of being duped, of sitting still for this long on this porch on the spot he had told her was going places, when her visions of him in the barn caring for minks, furs, and coats, dripped down onto the canvases which he actually kept there—coated with paint from gallons he bought at the Fine Paints Warner and brushed with colors mixed from pints and tubes—she thought herself capable of it.

And when she woke, just before opening her eyes, on those rare times she did dream that she could murder him, just before she remembered that he was already gone, that he had choked on a bay leaf and died, choking hard with her slapping his back and punching his stomach and trying, then, to save him, she said to herself, "Marilyn, you would do it all again. Don't fret. You know you would." And she meant taking him in the first place. And then, when she did remember he was gone and she wouldn't have to act out any passion, she meant trying to save him when she didn't know it was a bay leaf that was choking him.

She didn't know how much of a crime it was to sign Merle's canvases and mail them to the address that she had thought was a shipping company but was an art dealer, Rainbow Express, if the name she signed wasn't hers or Merle's and if the art dealer placed them in office buildings under the name he suggested she sign.

Bobby Joe's and Junior's reason for not wanting the officers on the porch, though on the porch was a damn sight better than in the barn, as Bobby Joe said to Junior in the front of the truck that he drove from the barn up the driveway, had to do with several days of fermentation before they could run what they were planning to label with canning labels, Mink Juice.

That Teedie knew it would be the sheriff on the porch and not his uncle and his mother, was not something Teedie told Marilyn now. He had actually pictured two police officers, remembering the city, and not a sheriff wearing a badge, and an officer with him.

"Bobby Joe and Junior," Teedie said to the sheriff and the officer who stood with their hands near their waists where they had, as Junior said later, the full arsenal.

The sheriff and the officer were not reaching down to pick up the iced tea Marilyn had poured them. Junior, leaning against the section of porch railing which Teedie had replaced, kept looking over his shoulder to where the space had been for so long that he didn't trust his weight.

Bobby Joe, leaning beside him, looked over his shoulder to see if the sheriff license tag was leaned up against the window in the truck. He couldn't tell and shifted his weight to move toward Junior on the railing and look again.

The cruiser, in blue colors with gold trim, was at the end of the driveway, parked crosswise up to the road fence posts where a radio shut on and off and made some electrical noise that no one on the porch could hear as words and which the officers ignored.

"We couldn't know where you were," the sheriff said, to no one in particular and so everyone jumped as his voice dropped onto them from the porch rafters, "and not know you would be here."

He brushed his hand along his belt and Junior, who had begun to think it wouldn't be a bad idea for the railing behind him to open up the same way it had when the Norton went through it at the place already cracked and weak where Marilyn—the day she wasn't now remembering—had let her end of the upside-down kitchen table drop onto it. He turned and saw the officer looking at him and lifted his hands from the railing to put into his pockets.

Bobby Joe, sliding toward him and trying to see over his other shoulder if the sheriff tag was visible in the truck, moved his ribs into Junior's elbow and jumped away and said, "Eew," and everyone looked at him.

"This shouldn't be a surprise to you," the sheriff dropped his voice from the porch rafters. Marilyn ran over again her dream of sliding along the wall behind the upholstered chair to reassure herself she hadn't done it and that he had to be accusing her of counterfeiting paintings she hadn't even done by herself and hadn't done at all for several years.

Junior tried to remember if any dancing he had done with Candy Adams against the back door at the Rod and Gun would get him into trouble with the law and tried to remember if she had said she was over eighteen.

Bobby Joe tried not to think about what was in the barn, about whether it was illegal to make the stuff or just to sell it, and about whether the quantity could work against him. Instead, he tried to think why on earth, when Junior had said, "You don't know how to make it," he hadn't listened. Or why, when it was obvious he would have to wait for rain and the cellar to fill, he hadn't just waited instead of leaving another white, lush spot where the refrigerator had been and fixing the refrigerator in the barn instead of water to run the coil through.

"The money, right here on this porch," the sheriff said. "The money. You know where it is?" and the thoughts of all of them leaped to a valise opened and full of pink and yellow paper bills.

Teedie looked at Marilyn who would not turn and look at the fountain and who said, onto the table, "Yes." Junior and Bobby Joe looked up at her and Teedie looked down at the floor.

"But it isn't here," she said.

The sheriff waited, his hands still, resting on his belt.

"I can get it."

"You?"

And she saw, from the little arcing motion Teedie drew with his toe across the porch floorboards in front of him, her mistake and said, "I can get it."

The sheriff waited. "It's taken this long," he said. "I can come back tomorrow, see every one of you here again, just the way I like it."

He reached a hand to the nearest iced tea and lifted the glass and drank.

"Course you could try to leave. Would make it slightly more difficult and a whole lot more incriminating."

He set down the glass and tugged up his belt and went down off the porch with the officer behind him.

Teedie started talking, low and fast, as soon as the officers dropped off the porch and Junior and Bobby Joe swung their legs over the porch railing and dropped into the ferns and sprinted to the barn. He started fast and low before Marilyn could ask him anything.

And Marilyn, from wondering whether they could arrest her, not for murdering Merle or for the false signatures on the paintings, but for possession of foreign money which

Merle had won illegally gambling a long time ago when he was alive, began to give her attention to Teedie.

Teedie was talking fast now and gesturing to let her know how much, very much, he had always thought of the mink ranch, how he had asked Merle right off for the job and had thought a lot about minks, but couldn't, of course, start a ranch of his own and so was happy to be in the town with one.

How he had thought, when he dozed off, late at night in his chair behind the desk they gave him in the maintenance department, that he could wake up a mink rancher and dreamt of the furry sleek creatures like a ferret he had seen once only rounder. How from his chair behind the desk, he directed the running of the mink ranch and at first he thought of the minks as coats for his grandmother, atonement for carrying her fortune out the apartment door when he was sixteen. But then he thought of them as people, animals, that is to say, and knew he would not ever make them into coats and when he ran the ranch it would be a terrible failure.

Marilyn put up her hand and he knew she meant to go back to the money, and without stopping or slowing, Teedie wheeled straight around and went back to the money, his hands making gestures on the air and erasing them and making others.

How the boy who was sixteen had thought—as the last of the family in the same country that the money was in—it was up to him to take the fortune which might be any amount of money in that country or this, he had no idea, and make it into a fortune in this country for the comfort of his grandmother and his mother and uncle. They would be surprised and pleased and he would tell them, then, because the grandmother would never look for the money in the knee wall in her apartment where everyone knew it was —and even if she did would find the note that he had it safe and would use it to accrue a fortune in his own right.

Except, he pedaled the air for breath . . . now it must have been, at this late date, his mother and his uncle who had found the note and set out to find what had become of him, which would mean that the grandmother had died without her mink coat which he wouldn't have let her wear anyway out of fondness for the minks.

Without trying to, Teedie looked exactly how sorry he had looked holding the flowers at his waist when he'd come to apologize for hitting her with the chair and Marilyn, the feel of milk coming into her breasts, reached across the lines and arcs and stars he was making in the air with his hands and touched his shoulders and pulled him to her. Teedie stopped erasing marks he had made and let his hands drop whatever it was he was trying to juggle to keep from falling and breaking against the floorboards, and leaned against her where he knew how to seek.

Bobby Joe and Junior backed the truck with plywood and two-bys into the driveway and watched the porch and the house. It was still light. Bobby Joe pushed in the clutch and let the truck idle. Junior slid out and went around and got the hammer from leaning against the post. The boat horn was on the table with bean vines and carrot tops and Queen Anne's lace Teedie had brought for the iced tea glass.

"Must have gone home," Junior said through the truck window.

Bobby Joe swiveled his neck to look out the back window and latched onto the steering wheel and backed the truck to the barn doors which Junior flung open.

The sound of minks down at the barn, setting up partitions around the water tank and refrigerator and tubing, sounded to Teedie, with his head on Marilyn's pillow and his eyes closed, like the sound of one of the boilers, and he caught himself from sliding into sleep. But then he remembered that the money had spilled the valise open, and he let himself slide into sleep.

Later, when it started to be dark and he heard the tiny metallic glitter of glass breaking and afterward the thud that must have preceded it, and Marilyn said, "Junior. Walked into that box of Christmas ornaments. From up-attic. For the fountain," he thought to call work and remembered it was his night off and put his arms around Marilyn and found, behind her on the bed, the soft curled animal that didn't move when he touched it. His first thought was mink and his second, just before he realized, was cat, and then he realized it was a wig, and Marilyn's own hair bit into his chest, and then he forgot again, everything except her and the bed that kept them from crashing onto the floor.

Marilyn, in deep night now, woke and looked at the ceiling and twisted out from under Teedie's arm and, softly, out over the edge of the bed which in her sleepiness still thudded around her. She didn't look to where Teedie had wrapped his hands around himself and lay curled into the pillow. She stepped over the jeans on the floor and, reminding herself that Junior, on the way in from the Rod and Gun, might have kicked the box of Christmas ornaments away from the foot of the stairs and into her path, moved carefully across the living room which she could see faintly in the outside light coming through windows.

Junior had shut the door and Marilyn opened it and stepped across the doorsill to the porch. The night breeze that skun around the corners of the barn skidded over her bare skin where Teedie had earlier. Marilyn lifted her arms and turned in the moving air and let it touch all of her and let her arms down to shoulder height, straight out, and balanced for a moment on air, before stepping down the porch step.

Then, from the fountain, she could see the white T-shirt he had pulled on with his jeans. She didn't stop what she was doing, taking the fountain apart, placing the ornaments onto the grass, and she didn't look at him again as he came up to her. Then she took hold of the tire on her side and did look at him and he took hold of the tire on the other side where it wasn't cemented to the one beneath and they lifted and set it on the grass.

Breeze from the barn reached around her, and she leaned into the fountain thinking, "If I'm wrong and they didn't put it here in the night, if that wasn't what I heard . . . the sheriff on the porch with the flowers in the tea glass . . ." She thought now that the noise could have been something to do with the still she thought they were working down in the barn, the still that she didn't want to know anything about so in case the sheriff and officer asked her she wouldn't be able to tell them, but then her hand touched and slid across the valise.

Breeze tingled off her shoulder blades. She thought she knew the money would be inside, they wouldn't . . . her hand slid to the handle and Teedie's slid over it.

"Whose money is this now?" Teedie said. "Right now."

And Marilyn stopped lifting on the handle where Teedie had his hand over hers, pushing it down.

"You won back half," she said. "Half of whatever there is—whatever it is worth. But . . ."

"Wait. Half of it is mine, yes? The half I won back and it may be worth millions, yes?"

"Or it may be worth nothing. In either case . . ." her hand was on the handle ready to lift the valise from the fountain.

"In either case, they wouldn't come after it so much in all these years if it were only worth a little. Never mind. I don't begrudge them. A half of it is mine. All of my life since I can remember, I have been dreaming of the mink ranch and I am here, now, in the middle of the night, asking if I can buy from you, not the mink ranch, I know I cannot, but half the mink ranch for whatever half of the money is worth."

"But . . ."

Whether Marilyn would have told him what she was about to tell him about minks would afterwards confuse her as she was confused at times about whether she had murdered Merle. She didn't tell him because Teedie, in an urgency she already associated with a boat horn, associated with his reaching across the sheet they had twisted to the floor and leaning his weight on her, said, and held her other arm, "Wait . . . don't," and she didn't know if he had somehow guessed.

"Don't tell me anything except yes or no," he said. "Yes, I may buy half of this mink farm and keep the job as well, of course, or no, I may have no part of the mink farm or here or whatever is on it. It is not for me."

And Marilyn saw he had her.

He did not brush his hands against her breasts then. He let go her arm and stayed very still. And then he tipped over the fountain with her, resting one shoulder against it to look at her in the soft dark nighttime light, and Marilyn didn't wait to answer, found his knee in the jeans and poked her finger through the soft frayed spot and said, "Yes," and moved her hand on the handle of the valise from under his to catch him as he leaned himself against her in the fountain and the Easter grass.

Bobby Joe, from dreaming about struggling with a sea serpent on his way to Treasure Island, stepped out of his room to the top of the stairs and reached his hand to the banister. As he touched it, something cold and slimy wrapped and clutched his bare ankle, and as he stepped his other foot back, tentacles of the huge briny sea-deep monster filling the hall behind him wrapped and clutched his other ankle.

Fear pounded to the top of his head and back to his toes. He clenched his eyes tight to squeeze white stars against his eyelids. Along with a panic he was about to feel, raced a hope that he was still asleep and dreaming and hadn't actually stepped to the top of the stairs. Then he felt the weight of something monstrous-heavy dragging itself to him by its hold on his ankles and he flung himself backwards from the top of the stairs and landed full-out in the hall. With the hall floor thumping through him, he waited to twist one way or the other against the grip on his ankles ready to drag him and hold him under long enough—however long it took—to stop him from breathing. And then the creature moved, and he twisted and took a breath and smelled beer, and Junior rolled on top of him and Bobby Joe pushed him off and leaped to his feet on the deck, still living.

He took in gulps of air that pounded through his body and he put his hands on his hips. Junior didn't move from where he'd been thrown off and Bobby Joe said, "What're you doing here? Lying on the floor in the middle of the night?"

"Sleeping."

"You shouldn't be sleeping at the top of the stairs. Anybody could trip over you and fall headfirst down the stairs and break his neck."

"That's why I grabbed you. Keep you from falling headfirst."

Bobby Joe still couldn't see Junior in the air that was darker than the air downstairs where light from outside came through the windows.

"Thanks," Bobby Joe said.

"What're you doing?"

"If you must know, I'm going down to get the money so we don't all land up in court or jail or something."

"Yeah?" Junior said. "I don't know. Why don't we just tell her where it is in the morning?"

"Well, look." Junior wasn't making any move to sit up and so Bobby Joe dropped down next to him. "She hasn't gone anywhere, right? Which means she's planning to go tomorrow and dig up the cemetery fountain so she'll have the money on the porch when they come for it."

Junior lifted a hand and let it thump onto the floor.

"So if we get it out of the fountain now, then she wouldn't ever have to know, would she, that we moved it in the first place? We could just let on that we knew when she took it to the cemetery and so here it is all dug up for her."

Bobby Joe could hear Junior pushing himself up off the floor and, when they were both standing, decided not to hit him here and now because of the noise it would make, decided to hold against him the experience of having his hair lifted off his head to leave a cool spot for the seawater to wash over.

Bobby Joe put his hand to the banister post again and waited, but nothing happened so he went downstairs and Junior followed and scuffed the last step.

The fountain didn't look as solid, heavy, as they remembered it. In air just changing from night to morning, light prickled around the fountain and a bird that started chirping in a tree let loose all the other birds hidden there. Junior and Bobby Joe crept to the fountain, one on each side, and put their hands onto the now familiar painted rubber tires which, up until the truck backed into them, they couldn't remember ever touching. They were just beginning to lift the mid tire when something big and heavy-seeming glided low from the trees right at them, heavy on the air as if to crush them and, with the cry of a sea monster, batted the air where their heads had been before they ducked, and lifted past the cat they saw—when they lifted their heads again—crouched at the edge of the porch roof above the stairs.

The cat lifted itself from the crouch and batted a paw into the air and crouched again in motion so fast that in the dizziness of first morning light they couldn't be sure they had seen it move at all. The bird pulled its weight and the trail of morning air over the roof and sank out of sight behind it.

Bobby Joe and Junior kept their heads down and lifted the top half of the fountain off the bottom half and set it on the ground and put their hands, two, three, four hands, into the empty space where—they looked across at each other to assure themselves—the valise had been.

Across the empty space their hands reached to their elbows and touched each other and leaped back and Bobby Joe and Junior looked up from the empty space where they could see the valise missing, saying in the same words to each other, "We did, didn't we? Put the money in here?" And each, seeing the stricken face of the other, nodding too much, too hard, answered, "Yes. I know we did."

"It was night," Bobby Joe said.

"And we dug it up at the cemetery."

"And it was covered with dirt," Bobby Joe nodded.

"And we brought it back here."

"And left it in the truck. Yes." Bobby Joe looked at the truck just coming out of the night air into morning at the end of the driveway.

"And came down at night," Junior said.

"And put it in."

Birds and trees fluttered and air picked up off the ground. "Yes," Bobby Joe said, "because we wouldn't both remember it the same."

"She's gonna kill us," Junior said.

"How could . . ." Bobby Joe looked again at the empty place in the fountain and then together they said, "Teedie."

"Won't be out of work yet," Bobby Joe said. They lifted the top half of the fountain onto the bottom half where it looked slightly crooked or caved-in.

"I'll put on my boots," Bobby Joe said. "We'll meet him there."

"I slept in mine," Junior said.

"I noticed." Bobby Joe stepped up the step to the porch. Junior followed him, and the cat, tipped over the edge and waiting, dropped from the porch roof onto Junior's shoulders, and Junior completed his step onto the porch, grabbed the boat horn off the table, and pressed the button. The cat leaped in the kind of splayed-out motion cats leap in cartoons, with all four feet at the same time, off Junior's shoulder, landed behind him on the porch floor, and, already running before it hit, bolted for the barn.

The sound of the boat horn that lifted Marilyn and Teedie, wrapped around each other with Teedie's jeans underneath, off the bed and flopped them back down, shattered them from the other side of sleep to this and rang around the walls of the room several times. Marilyn's heart was pounding so fast, and she could feel Teedie's so fast that she thought that maybe what had been happening on the other side of sleep had been happening with Teedie awake and alert beside her. And Teedie thought that Marilyn had been awake that way, and rolled with her onto his back, and she pushed him firmly and repeatedly back down into the bed so that when she stopped and merely lay against him, holding him down with her weight, he didn't move at all.

W hatever dreams Adley Walker-Stanton had been having at Foley's Brass Mill before being lifted out of his chair behind the desk his feet were still on, escaped him as he tried to free one or the other elbow enough to tip the hat off his face and see Junior on one side of him and Bobby Joe on the other.

First he thought they wouldn't let him down, arched as he was from where they were holding him above the chair to where his feet were on the desk, and then, when they saw him without the hat over his face, he was afraid they would drop him and pedaled the air with his elbows as much as he could in their grips. They set him into the chair and he swung his feet down off the desk.

"All right," Bobby Joe said.

Junior said, "Where is he?" as if Adley Walker-Stanton had taken someone and hidden him.

Bobby Joe said, "Teedie."

"Oh." Adley Walker-Stanton straightened in the chair. "Night off."

The room was suddenly empty of everyone except himself and he reached for the phone and dialed the number for the boilers.

"All right," Bobby Joe said and they got into the truck and drove to Jake's package store, where the ice machine stood quietly important and leaked water across the concrete and onto the parking lot, and Bobby Joe turned off the truck and stillness wrapped around them.

"All right. What we'll do is, we'll knock on the door," Bobby Joe said.

They went between the weeds down the path to the small house.

"All right. Stand back," Bobby Joe said, as if Teedie would burst through the doorway once he opened the door and saw them standing there and head straight for the West Coast if he hadn't already done so, which, it seemed, judging by the quiet, perhaps he had.

Light gathered into warmth around them and Bobby Joe reached his knuckles again across still space and rapped them against the door.

Quiet of the empty house seeped through cracks around the door. Bobby Joe reached again and stillness behind them broke into morning and became the sound of the ice machine generator, and Bobby Joe opened the door and they waited. They looked inside and, without stepping over the doorsill, Bobby Joe reached the door and pulled it closed.

"Don't worry," Junior said. "I have it all figured out."

Bobby Joe said, "I can imagine." He dropped the truck into gear and backed out of Jake's.

"No, listen. What we need is diversion. You know, something that if things aren't going just right, we can use to take their minds off..."

"Look. What they said is they want the money. No charges. No questions."

"All right. But what are we going to give them for the money if Teedie has it?" Junior said. "Or if, just for instance, we think Teedie has it but, however, somebody else—completely foreign outside the family that we don't know—came and took it out of the fountain and is right now just living it up out on the West Coast, probably riding a Norton 750 to do it."

"All right. Now listen. There's still a chance Teedie has it and what we have to do, we have to find Teedie and make him lead us to the money. So all right."

Junior said, "But if he doesn't, I mean. What we'll need is a diversion. Unless you want to see all of us dragged off in chains."

Bobby Joe crossed his elbows over the steering wheel and uncrossed them pulling into the driveway.

"She's maybe walked out to the cemetery," Junior said when they didn't see Marilyn on the porch.

"She maybe hasn't gotten up yet, either," Bobby Joe said and left the truck and climbed inside the house to finish sleeping.

W|hen Bobby Joe heard the voices on the porch and
saw through the window the cruiser at the end of
the driveway, he put on his Davy Crockett hat and went
down the stairs with the idea of being closer to the barn
in case he had to defend it and closer to the truck in case
he had to use it, and stopped quickly with his foot over
the doorsill when he saw the valise on the table.

His foot above the doorsill made the motion of a couple
quick jabs to the gas pedal and everyone looked at it before
he put his foot down. "Morning. Didn't expect you this
early is all," he said and looked past them at the barn to
see if he could see Junior and give him the wave that
everything was all right. But the barn doors were closed
and the near window propped open with the hammer.

"All right, then," the sheriff said.

He looked toward the barn and Bobby Joe thought he
should have dismantled the still and put it away before
they came back.

Something leaped out the barn window and Teedie
thought it was an escaped mink and didn't know whether
to root for it or try to catch it before he realized it was the
cat which streamed between them on the porch and into
the house, and they heard it next on the roof of the porch
and from the barn again came a noise not metal . . .

"What," the sheriff said, "is that?" And they all turned
their heads from looking up at the porch rafters for the
cat toward the barn where the noise, not completely
human, or animal, or birdlike—though it reminded Teedie
of a birdcall his uncle used to have made of plastic, half
orange and half yellow, with a half yellow, half orange bird
perched on top with notes embossed in the plastic—began
again across space and air.

The noise a train might make braking on rusty nails,
Bobby Joe thought, the noise they had made, when they
were kids and had pumped the porch swing to sound like

the train pulling into the station and he would make Junior drop off the swing and check the oil and grease the wheels and then holler, "All 'board," and pump the swing again moving end to end, not back and forth, with Junior in the caboose.

"A sick mink," he said and everyone turned to him and he shrugged his shoulders and pulled the Davy Crockett hat onto his forehead. "Junior's down there. It's all right." He leaned against the railing.

The sound of Junior, lying on his back on the floor, warbling mink impersonations at the ridgepole of the barn came through the open barn window. Bobby Joe leaned against the unpainted part of the railing and, though he was sure now that he did not have the sheriff sign in the windshield, he wasn't so sure he could keep himself from looking backwards over his shoulder. And lightning through him, Bobby Joe leaped off the railing and thought, in an instant, putting two and two together, what he should have thought before—why hadn't he?—of the sheriff license plate and what Bosco must have meant, "Your father'd get a kick out of having that plate." Looking backwards, he knocked himself forward against the table at a height that made him double over and turn his head just in time to snap his face into the bouquet of flowers that Teedie had brought, tiger lilies that Bobby Joe thought he must have weeded around several lifetimes ago in Jeannetta Tillotson's garden, and sprang back again, and with everyone on the porch now looking at him said, "Excuse me. Some help. Junior." And, trying to walk sideways around the pain crimped in the front of him, stepped down the steps onto the driveway toward the barn.

"All right, then," the sheriff said again. "I'm satisfied that you've delivered what we came for, none the worse for wear."

Marilyn stepped onto Teedie's foot, and he covered his face with his hands and rubbed a grin down off his cheekbones. And Marilyn carefully did not look at him, thinking that the picture of Teedie covered with pink and yellow foreign money where she had licked his skin wet and stuck the bills to him was so clear to her that the sheriff and the officer must see it and the trail of bills to the valise, open on the floor, and the way the bills fell off one or more at a time as Teedie dried and rubbed against her.

On the porch they heard the sound of some sort of glitter breaking, perhaps against cages, and sparking out through the near window that was propped open with the hammer. Sunlight caught the sparks and turned them and dropped them on the grass and more sparks shot out.

The sheriff looked at Marilyn and Marilyn smiled and said, "My guess would be Christmas ornaments. He walked into a box of them last night."

"Yes, ma'am," the sheriff said and put his hand around the handle of the valise and let its weight slide off the table and rest against his leg and motioned with his head to the officer, Let's get outta here, and the officer followed him down off the porch at a quick run to the cruiser.

"You don't want to know," Marilyn said to Teedie and took his hand and pulled him off the porch and inside.

"You let him get that going—if that's what I think it is down there with the minks that they don't want us to see," the sheriff said to the officer in the passenger seat. "What you want to do is let him get that going, if that is what he has down there, get everything implicated, and then, when he does a run, what he'll do is give it to Jake to sell for him. Then, you want to come take a look. Not now. No. You want to . . ."

He drove the cruiser. "You see how he ducked down off the porch? Now you put that together with yesterday how they're throwing looks over their shoulders like something's ready to leap out and get them and you start thinking, Maybe it should be me. What is it they've got going down there?"

It wasn't Teedie's idea to go to the fair. It was too hot and threatening rain and, standing in front of the row of stacked rabbit cages by the sign KEEP HANDS AWAY FROM CAGES, he couldn't remember whose idea it was. Marilyn held his elbow in front of the cages, where exactly what he wanted to do was put his fingers through the mesh to touch the soft moving fur and the droopy tender ears.

When he had had as much as he wanted of not being able to touch the rabbits, and of wondering if he would ever touch the minks—which seemed always beyond his grasp—he went with Marilyn to look at the flower arrangements and at the jams and jellies and cakes, pies, peppers, squash, kale he couldn't touch either that had won or lost in competitions.

Outside the tents of displays were merry-go-round music and a space shuttle that rotated and moved up and down and a Ferris wheel, silent except the motion of the hanging seats, clicking to rise and fall and circle and thrust legs out before them and pull them back.

Grass on the midway was pounded dusty and hot and, from the booths they walked past, men or women in T-shirts called to them, "Five for a dollar, take a shot, won't you? For the little lady here?"

At the livestock rink where oxen were pulling weights on a stone boat and a backhoe was hauling the stone boat back, Junior was leaning his elbows onto his knees in the bleachers, watching.

Bobby Joe, with his Davy Crockett hat pulled onto his forehead, stood with his elbow propping the BB gun and aimed at the tin ducks gliding across the back wall of the booth and falling off the end of the line to go upside down behind the shelf and come up again at the end of the line crossing in front of his sights. He was wondering, like a shadow on his left shoulder, whether an officer of the law had right and privilege to go into a person's barn while the person was not at home, was at the fair shooting ducks, for instance, on suspicion of there being a still on the property.

He was wondering, like a cold hand on his left shoulder, whether just owning a put-together still and having it set up on the property was enough to constitute breaking the law.

What spun him around to look behind him and remember where he was and look across the midway where the nearest people standing still were Teedie and Marilyn, was wondering whether having a put-together still, and beer making, and seven gallons of whiskey that Merle had made in glass jars in the barn cellar under the still constituted a . . .

Twilight and rain clouds folded eerily around the rides and, at the edge of the road, around the maple trees where the lights threw shadows up into the leaves.

Junior was sitting in the truck cab when they came to it, watching car headlights spring across the field and the cars follow them. Sky folded onto the roofs of the cars and trucks and dropped between them onto the grass.

In the headlights, each blade of grass, dusty and driven-over, had a shadow that propped it up.

Rain wasn't coming down yet from the thunderheads toward home. Junior leaped from one foot to the other in the back of the truck, sliding against the cab to rock it while it was moving, and slamming his hands down onto the roof of the cab and singing so they could hear whatever wasn't whipped backwards away from him by the motion of the truck or whatever stayed in the same place while Bobby Joe drove him forward out from under it, "I Gave the Phone My Nickel, but It Didn't Give Me You."

In the cab, sitting next to the door, Teedie had his hand across his waist to Marilyn's waist and under her stretchy pullover with her breasts resting on it. Bobby Joe watched the road to drive the truck between it and the sky. And they all saw, at the same time, the crack of lightning across grey dull cloud and the hit of thunder that swerved the truck—unless it was Junior shifting his weight or Marilyn moving her elbow into Bobby Joe's side—and Bobby Joe said what they were thinking, "That was ours. It hit the house," and pulled the truck faster so that Junior lay his chest across the roof of the cab and lifted his face into the wind and let his hands flap time beside it, and Marilyn said, what they hadn't thought of yet, "Lucky you weren't in it."

They weren't so far away that, when they came to the end of the driveway and Bobby Joe crossed his elbows to turn in, they couldn't see the hot bright spring of fire from the ridgepole of the barn to the foundation, a sheath of fire siding that ran up in flames, that made waves lifting off the roof, and feel in the truck the concussion of air from all of the barn on fire at once in the instant that the lightning touched it.

Bobby Joe stopped the truck next to the fountain.

Before the rain, in the night, hit the dust on the driveway and rolled it into balls and spattered down the porch roof to land in the ferns and flapped down shiny over the hot and missing timbers and the stone foundation, the barn held the flames.

At first they couldn't get near it. In the matter of minutes it took the barn to consume itself and collapse like fireworks, Teedie and Marilyn and Junior watched from the porch.

Bobby Joe, in the driveway next to the truck, could feel the tender breeze blowing heat off the still, what was twisted left of it, and off the heated foundation, blowing soft-looking sparks off softened wood and ruins of paint cans.

And now they still didn't move to go down, could see what they needed to see from where they were.

Bobby Joe pushed off the truck and went up the porch steps. He stopped thinking that it was a sign that he wasn't to be a distiller of liquors and maybe get himself arrested and dragged off the porch and past the fountain —which he didn't even like much but would miss in the grey cell where they put him—and started to be angry about the loss of equipment and the work he'd invested.

He forgot that it was Junior he was supposed to let walk first across the darkened living room and went across himself. What surprised him—as he reached his hand for the banister, tripped into the upholstered chair he had moved to the foot of the stairs so that the weight of the chair collapsing under him over the missing back leg tugged the rope he'd bought for the truck, which pulled the box he had found putting the Christmas ornaments up-attic fast to the edge of the landing where it stopped abruptly against the cleat he had nailed there and hurled two dozen imitation minks in the form of Davy Crockett hats down the stairs around him—was not the minks themselves. What surprised him was the intense sound which screamed off the walls and ceiling, slamming him flat into the chair, raising the hair on his head, and cramming his heartbeats hard together, of Junior, standing in the doorway, holding his thumb hard down on the button for the boat horn.

ABOUT THE AUTHOR

Randeane Tetu is trying to learn to ice skate. Her stories don't reflect this at all. Several of her stories have received national awards for fiction. "Depth of Field" is listed in *The Best American Short Stories, 1989.* Her work has appeared in many magazines and anthologies, including the 1991 American Booksellers Association Honors Book, *When I Am an Old Woman I Shall Wear Purple* (Papier-Mache Press, 1987).

About the Artist

Leif Nilsson was born in Conecticut in 1962. He was classically trained as an artist in Europe, New York, and Old Lyme, CT. He lives with his wife Katherine in Chester, CT, where he maintains a studio. He is represented by Summa Gallery in New York and Inglis Art in San Francisco.